THE ROT

THE SUNKEN PLACE

AND GRACE

FRANCISCA SERRETTE

ACKNOWLEDGEMENTS

To Courtney, who I will continue to love from afar. To my father, who I love beyond this life and to my mother, who I love in spite of it all. To my friends and my children and all those who have supported my journey. To those who took the time to read these pages while they were being conceived and to my ride or dies, Laws, Cuzzy, Soph and Keers.

To all those mentioned in the book: Please know that this is not a derogatory account of you as a person, but that it is simply information from my perspective. There still remains the 99 percent of the other versions of you. I honour them all. This book is not a slight on you. Thank you for process, the learning, the trials, the tribulations, and the wisdom you have afforded me. Don't be offended, please allow my experience of you to offer guidance and wisdom to others in need.

Don't take it personally; I don't. I love you, and I am thankful for everything in my life.

And finally, thank you to my God. To your God. By whatever name and by whatever form you wish to call this universal intelligence, consciousness, source energy, unknown, Pacha Mumma, wind, esoteric wisdom, quantum matter in the quantum field. Thank you.

And to Jesus. Who undoubtably saved my life that night.

CONTENTS

1. Acknowledgments — II
2. Preface — V
3. 17 JUNE 2020 — 1
4. WHAT IF, ONE — 12
5. 22 JUNE 2020 — 42
6. WHAT IF, TWO — 44
7. 25 JUNE 2020 — 63
8. WHAT IF, THREE — 67
9. 30 JUNE 2020 — 79
10. WHAT IF, FOUR — 82

11. 5 JULY 2020   103

12. WHAT IF, FIVE   107

13. 13 JULY 2020   125

14. WHAT IF, SIX   131

INTERMISSION: THE FOUR EASY-PEASY STEPS TO KNOWING THAT YOU MIGHT POSSIBLY BE POSSESSED

- ADMIT THERE'S A PROBLEM
- ADMIT THAT THE PROBLEM IS NOT EVERYONE ELSE
- ADMIT THAT THE PROBLEM IS, IN FACT, YOU
- ADMIT THAT, IN TRUTH, IT'S NOT YOU, AT ALL

15. AND GRACE . . .   167

16. 16 JANUARY 2021   174

PREFACE

I write this memoir not in ode to me and my many triumphs and tribulations, but mainly, I write as a partial bystander to much of it all; large sections channelled and downloaded – myself an avid spectator to much of what is written here. So much so, the editing process seemed to me more like reading it for the first time.

At first my journal entries were to simply record my experiences, as much of it I did not wish to forget – it being a completely unexpected and absolutely unbelievable occurrence. I did not expect to easily hold onto my experiences in memory, PTSD setting in in the immediate aftermath.

I write this memoir to bring into the light the long-forgotten principles around Good and evil, the long-suppressed truth of entity attachment and how we dismiss and undermine our own people in their struggles with it. The knowledge of just how real the real is: We are not alone in this spiritual warfare. We are not alone in this dimension, in either the incarnation of the devil, Lucifer and his many minions, or in the power of God, Jesus and his many angels. And ultimately us.

I don't seek to scare or petrify you, or to be a fearmonger. I simply wish to bring to your attention forces beyond our vision that nonetheless have grave influence over our actions, our hearts and our souls. It is only in the knowledge of this that we can fight back and support others and their own internal, external, and supernatural battles. It is only with this awareness that we can love our children, ourselves, one another and ultimately the dark to bring it into the light. Because we are the light.

17 June 2020

So, there I find myself. Weak and tempted. Midnight, and I'm violently throwing up. Forcefully coming up from the MDMA and the cocktail of all the other drugs raging through my system. But unlike every other time I have vomited my high. This time, for the first time, I call on Him. I pray to Him. To calm me. To pull me through. And despite convulsing. Violently convulsing. I stand. Arms open. Hands up. Face to the sky. Waves of beauty and sickness washing over me. Showering down on me. Crashing and breaking. Drawing back, only to engulf me again. In a breath-taking nausea.

So I drag myself together and venture back downstairs. And this is what I remember:

Another bump of ketamine. And immediately falling. Surrendering. Abandoning myself. Into a loop. A hole. A black hole. A void from which I can observe my own vacance. Harrowed and absent. But we all felt it. The energy in the room changes. We all began searching for comfort. For reassurance. In the world. In each other. Worried glances and expressions of fear covering our faces. Suddenly and desperately terrified, I grab my beloved's arm. Fingers digging deep into his flesh. Vicelike. Desperate. And desperately begging. Beseeching him. Searching the room. For an answer. For protection. To know what was happening.

Spirals. Spirals of grey plumes. Shooting and shooting down. Down and down. And down. Into malicious and sinister points. Daggering into the space around us. Menacingly close. And I knew it. I knew it immediately. That they were coming for us. I tried. I really tried. In my compromised state. To reach out. To warn him. And I know, right then, without a shadow of a doubt, that we needed protection.

***

For as long as I can remember I have suffered. I have been tormented. Painful thoughts. Hurtful. Scornful. Hateful and bitter. Hate to myself. Hate to everyone. Greed, envy, judgement and disgust fill my head. Every waking hour. And plague me in my dreams. And a rot. A rot that has been there for as long as I can remember. Lives in my abdomen. A twisting, curling hand that emanates constant pain. A pain pinpointed to a pinprick of agony. And an agony so strong, it radiates throughout me.

I have hated myself. I have hated all those who loved me. And, mostly, I have hated God. I couldn't hear His name without being repulsed. And though I wanted desperately to know Him, to commune with Him, the mention of Him causes me to shudder. Like nails on a chalkboard. The sound of His name. The thought of His love. Sets my soul on edge. I am wretched. Sure that God does not love me. That I am not special to Him. And that He certainly did not care to save me.

My partner and the love of my life has been hanging on for dear life. Giving his all, his body, his mind and his soul for my salvation. Two and a half long years. Battling alone. Carrying us. Trying to find the cure. To this plague. Counselling, medication, meditation, psilocybin, micro-dosing, exercise, love, compassion, motivation, anger, despair and desperation. All ineffective. And I remain. Hateful. Refusing to be loved. Blaming him for all the wretched hatred I have for myself. Pushing him away and hating him and myself for it.

He found God so many years ago and has his own miracle to call on. To know unwaveringly. He exists. And loves him more than could be expressed. And I hate him for it. And I hate Him for it.

I have been dying slowly. I have decided it is time. To end it. I have been making plans. How to say goodbye to my loved ones. How to say sorry. How to confess my failure. I am failing everyone. Everyone around me. They will be better off. I have been planning. How to record my farewell messages. And I have been crying. For the pain I will cause my children. But I know. Ultimately. That this is best for them.

I have been wrestling with whether God will forgive me, and I can still go to heaven. Because He knows how tortured I am. How trapped within myself I feel.

I go to see my friend. Two hundred and forty miles just to say goodbye. Or perhaps to save myself. I have lost track. I collect a car I don't even need. A spontaneous action followed by a spontaneous event. I pack it to return home. A midnight venture. Blankets and pillows provided. The weighted blanket a present for my autistic son. Or my depressed alter ego. I decide against taking my children with me to hell in a flurry of indignation. So I drive with the sun to guide me.

By Sunday evening I'm back home and fighting to find reason. Reasons to hold on to life. Wanting to end it all. But I am without courage or conviction. Instead, I find myself driving the streets of my hometown. Instinctively knowing, the car stops, so do I. I am exhausted. Of everything. Of life. Of pain. Of feeling apart from myself. And God. And everyone else. Of being convinced that I am worthless.

I am tired of the voices in my head. And the hate in my heart. And the rot. Bubbling and churning at the centre of me. I have been wanting to go. I want to go now.

Some weeks beforehand I had gone to a small gathering. Sat around the fire I listened to the harrowing, amazing story of an exorcism. Sat there. Intent. Sceptical and scathing. Knowing it was both crazy and deranged and real. And true. Something touching at the corners of my soul. Something rousing me. Something I can't quite touch. Ignorant and scared, yet captivated and intrigued. Yearning. Leaning in. Alit. Tentatively awakened.

It was with this in mind my love had prayed to Jesus. Beseeched Him. Begged Him to remove what he felt was a bad spirit. A negative oppression on his soul. He tells me of his experience. The feeling of being liberated. Of crying uncontrollably. And the instantaneous relief that floods through him.

Much to my dismay, my shock and my awe. My love brings to me an excerpt, a talk, a teaching, a sermon. On demons. A video about demons. And a pastor. Who had suffered depression for years with no cure. Speaking of how the simplicity of knowing. Really knowing that these behaviours. These thoughts. These feeling. These things. Were not you. That this was eighty percent of the battle. Eighty percent of the battle. The battle?

Something has resonated in me. Something deep down. Something unconscious and asleep. Something on the periphery. Something I wasn't even aware was lost. Resonates in me. And the familiar feeling of rot twists and turns in my stomach. In silent angst. In silent fear. And having never believed in fairy tales and demons. Good and evil. God or the devil. I know. And I understand.

I have spent the rest of my day screaming. With every fibre of my being. In Jesus' name. That this thing is not welcome. Not anymore. Asking that God cast it out. Every time I have felt that rot bubbling. In its venture to cause me pain. Make me hateful. I have prayed. I have prayed to God. And renounced the devil. I have told it clearly. It has been seen. It can no longer hide from the light. That this soul belongs to God. That it has nowhere to go. It has been rumbled. And it needs to get the fuck out.

By the end of the day. By the time I lay my head down to sleep. I am already feeling better. More loving. More patient. Strangely more at home. Despite not knowing where I have been. The saturation in the world has been cranked up. And the rot has been dialled down. By this evening when our friend comes to visit. I am feeling more awake than I ever have. Confused as to what slumber I had been under.

I have promised I will not take drugs today. Tonight. When our friend arrives. But I am weak and tempted. And so there I find myself.

***

I jerk. Back in the room. Red-rimmed eyes and scared features searching it. Awakened from where? Disappeared momentarily. Now straddled on top of my love. My vice-like grip transferred to his shoulders. His back. His face. Holding on tightly. For dear life. Roused from somewhere else. By a voice. Telling me. Imploring me. Urging me to let go. In a desperate, urgent whisper. I open my mouth. A sound eerily familiar pushes itself out of me. An unholy exhale from deep, deep inside. And again. Momentum building. Like that same wave. In a mighty storm. Pulling back. Only to unleash itself.

To engulf all those who stand and face it. Crashing down, the sound drives itself out. Brutally. Forcefully. Painfully. My abdomen hard clenched from the exertion. The voice again. Screaming at me. Calling through the commotion. To let go. To let go! And as I do, my head shoots up; body rigid, mangled, twisted and misshapen. Mouth wide and gapping.

Moments pass. Maybe hours. And all I hear. From the depths of my oblivion. The quiet of my nothingness. From this sunken place. Is the word 'Jesus'. Whispered into my ear. By a voice so close I can touch it. And a mouth so familiar I can feel it. But from a place far, far away. Yet spoken so loudly it deafens me. And I watch. In my mind's eye as a grey shadow. Dark as translucent gunmetal. Intangible and discarnate. Yet as real as my very own flesh. Rips itself from inside of me. Gathered up. From my arms, my legs. From the tips of my fingers and the depths of my soul. Gathered up and poured, expelled and vomited out of my mouth. The very last of it rooted to my stomach, to my abdomen. Where the rot dwells. Latched on so strongly that it tears itself with such force my body begins to convulse.

And just like that. Just like that. I know. It is gone. The root of it dragged out of my body so viciously I collapse. Weak and exhausted.

My body can feel itself being laid down. Empty. See-through. Almost as if you could pass your hand straight through it. And I, a witness. Witness from that same spot. From the space in my abandoned abdomen. The space where the rot dwelled. Now empty and fragile. White layers of light. Filling me up. Like the lights being turned on in an abandoned warehouse. Section by section. And my body, in time, pulsating. Reverberating. Throbbing out the light. Pulsing beauty, in the form of blinding white fireworks. Thrusting from my body. In the rhythm of my quickened heartbeat, beating itself into delirium. With what can only be described as pure grace. With what could only be but the light of God. Shining out of my fingers. My body full to the brim. So full it is fit to burst. The love of God. Overwhelming me. Taking me. Taking me back to Him.

What beauty. What mercy. What privilege. To be carried away. By Him. To be leaving this earth. Touching the heavens, only inches from the ground. Gracefully surrendering. Gratefully dying. From the all-consuming force being just minimally closer to Him brings.

I can feel Him. All around me. Inside of me. Bursting out of me. And I can't bear it. Somewhere in the distance I can hear my love calling for me. But I am fading. Immobilized by the power of the pure, beautiful, unadulterated love that being just this much closer to God is. I find the strength. And somehow the inspiration to call for the weighted blanket. Somewhere in my haze comprehending its vitality. Instinctively knowing it will weigh me down. And anchor me back to the Earth. I can hear them now. Panicked and scared, running to save my life. Somehow intrinsically aware of the gravity. The urgency. The reality of this situation.

The minute the blanket is placed over me everything slows. I can breathe. Taking long, slow, vigorous gulps. Vitality reaching my lungs and spreading throughout my body. Oxygen and life carried to each cell. Reaching my heart. Which in turn begins to beat more steadily. Evenly. Determinedly. My body only just bearing this power. This power flowing through me. Subsiding from the raging river it once was, to more steady waters as it begins to calm.

And it is in this moment. This moment. The overwhelming nature of God now dissipated. That I begin to travel. Venture out. Simultaneously courageous and effortless. Through my own body. Noting veins and translucent muscle. I can see my flesh. From the inside. Pink and stretched. Feel myself floating through. And up and up. Into my face, into my mind, and finally into my eyes. I blink. Slowly and carefully. Opening them. My own eyes. For what I know is the first time in decades. The light of the room, the same room I had happily sat in only minutes beforehand, blinding me from the tenderness of sight. Like a newborn. Or a blind man cured.

All I can muster is a tentative 'hi'. Polite and timid in my address of the room. The room I have only just entered. Shy and reborn as myself. Coming back into the world again. For the first time in as long as I can remember.

Sitting there. On that sofa. Drained and bedraggled, the weighted blanket still wrapped around me. My body resonating from the force of being so close to God. Sitting there, I am hit again. A direct hit to the chest. To my heart. My soul. And I wail. I wail with joy. With pure joy. Weeping so passionately it cries out silently from my lips. Praising God and knowing I am indeed filled. Filled with the Spirit. That I was indeed saved. That I am indeed loved. I have never felt such pure bliss. Happiness. Grace. Euphoria. Ecstasy. I am in bliss. I am bliss. So overcome, all I can do is praise and wail and pray and thank and bow to the miracle I have just received.

***

Afterwards, my partner told me that whilst straddled to him. After crying out. After my body bolted upright, twisted and statuesque. He watched on in horror. As my demeanour calmed and my head came down. Purposefully. Eerily. And that he had looked directly into the eyes of a demon. It looked straight at him. Its face contorted into a vicious smile. Its lips tight and grimacing. Its eyes bulbous and swollen. And rolling back in my head. Covered by a grey film. My soul gone from behind them and my skin grey and thinned. Deathlike. He watched on in horror as it made nothing but fiendish, demonic grunts. Growling and staring at him with menace. And him. Calling my name and seeing I had left. And frightened only for me and my soul. Bolstered by his faith in the Almighty. Knew then that he had to call on the name of our Lord and Saviour. To drag this thing out of me. And with his faith. And the power of God. Faced the Devil. And saved my life.

And it is because Jesus' name is so powerful. That within a day and half. A demon. A person who had inhabited my body. My mind. My soul. For over twenty-five years. Because Jesus' name is so powerful. It was made powerless. Powerless and fleeing for its life.

And God Is Good.

What if, One

WHAT IF, 1) *IT DIDN'T TAKE AN EXORCISM TO WAKE YOU UP? IF THE TOXIC RELATIONSHIPS, THE ASSAULTS AND THE DRUGS, THE DEPRESSION AND THE PATHOLOGY WERE THE REAL FAÇADE. AND THE TRUTH WAS SOMETHING MUCH, MUCH SINISTER?*

WHAT IF YOU PULLED BACK THE VEIL TO REVEAL THAT GOOD AND EVIL ACTUALLY EXISTED? WHAT IF YOU WOKE UP AND REALISED WHO'S SIDE YOUR IGNORANCE HAD CHOSEN FOR YOU?

WOULD YOU CHOOSE AGAIN?

I had originally met Courtney aged twenty-one. By that point I already had one child, having him aged nineteen, following the abortion of a rape baby. I had somehow ended up with the distorted reality that this termination had been my fault and I therefore didn't have the luxury of using abortion as a contraceptive.

I had never really had much preparation for sex, this never being discussed in any meaningful way in my household, and by the time I was eighteen and pregnant had suffered multiple sexual exploitations and abuses. From the persistent boy with his fingers in me on the delipidated sofa at the age of twelve, to the old men with their skin-crawling comments and subsequent verbal abuse if I didn't politely blush, to my father's blame of my skirt length after being slammed up against the door of my East London house, words escaping my mouth. Leading eventually to the humiliation of lying silently back aged sixteen whilst a man ten years my senior goaded me to move him, "if I was strong enough".

About six weeks after I had been convinced by all those around me to suck my living child out of me, my mum violently attacked me. I had been pleading with her to leave me alone. She was convinced I was prostituting myself. For weed. So it's no surprise that two days after my eighteenth birthday I was politely asked to leave her house.

I had had no idea how to protect or respect myself or what it truly meant to be loved or demand love from others. I was at sea with my body and at sea with my mind. So by twenty-one when I met Courtney, I was somehow both damaged goods and childhood innocence. We met through his brother, who I had been sleeping with. Another person exploiting my silent submission as an opportunity to use me.

It was New Year's Eve 2006. I was now twenty-two, and he had just turned seventeen but looked and carried himself like a grown man. He left his prepubescent-looking friends and followed me into our local. We danced, we laughed, we sat under the stars, we kissed. It was electric. I got spiked and couldn't stand up or open my eyes. He left believing I had lodged him for a better offer, and I was rescued and carried home by my best friend and her forty-year-old boyfriend. Devasted, I woke the next morning feeling like a massive opportunity had slipped through my fingers, but not understanding why.

After this we didn't see each other for a few months. At our first meeting I tentatively asked him if he recalled any of the events of New Year's Eve, his pride preventing him from engaging with me and his jealousy causing him to be cruel. I was devastated. Still, somehow, we managed to navigate a friendship based on smoking weed and watching films. The attraction between us was obvious and the electricity palpable. It was unsurprising that we started sleeping with each other, sex being the only expressive language of care or love that either of us knew.

I initiated it. I wanted him. I wanted him to prove to myself I could. That I was better than all the other girls. That he needed me to affirm him as much as I needed him. But the thing is, despite his desperate glances, his stutters and his unspoken feelings, I never really had him, and my heart broke every time he returned to his 'real' girlfriend and for every other girl I knew he was sleeping with.

Despite spending hours and days and weeks together, after eighteen months I finally left. His real girlfriend was pregnant, and I couldn't bear any more heartache. I spent the last two hours of our relationship counselling him in his despair at the prospect of bringing life into this world, and I left knowing that I would never be able to have him in the way I craved. About a week later he hunted me down at a friend's house, quietly frantic at my departure from his life. He wants to be friends. I couldn't think of anything worse. Quietly watching on while he played home with another. Knowing that I wasn't crazy in believing that he felt something for me that was real and strong and complete.

That it was just us that was incomplete.

So, I moved on. Really in the only way I knew how. Rebounding into the sadistic arms of another. A man who would quickly become the father of my second son and a relationship that ruined me more than the one before.

It's funny how little you can know of someone, how cruel someone can turn out to be, when you're searching for reassurance about your worth in the world. When you're in desperate need of comfort. Desperate to know you mean something. Somewhere. To someone. When your whole relationship is based upon the desperate hope that this person wants you more than the last one ever did. More than your parents ever did.

Except he wanted me too much.

So much so that no one else could have or talk to me.

He locked me in his porch once. Right at the beginning. I should've known better, but in my desperate nativity I took it for love. For passion. I was so desperate to be loved, to be wanted, to be coveted, that I stayed. Soaking up the vanity that came with being needed that much.

As always, I had no one. No one to protect me. No one to guide me. No one to help or support me. And certainly no one who cared. I received nothing but sneering disdain from my mother and a crescendo of 'I told you sos' in my multiple hours of need. And my father was, as always, absent. Silently watching on with no real commitment to my happiness or my life. So I navigated the pitiful sham that was my relationship with a pride that bordered on arrogance.

Purposely blind to the humiliation I was allowing myself to be subjected to. Because how do you even begin to master humility when everyone around you thinks you're worthless anyway? How can you be more humbled than to know that no one cares?

And where was God?

Emulating the only fatherly role I knew? That of silent nothingness? I didn't even ask. I pushed on in a whirlwind of pain. Trapped and shaken in a soundless storm. Sick from the endless rain. Scared by the lightning that struck too close for comfort and deafened by the thunderous bellows of a man that hated to love me. Asking no one for help.

Depressed, cheated on, beaten up, mentally tortured and falling slowly into madness, I brought my newest child into this world. I disliked him from the moment he was born. I didn't know him. Or own him. He wasn't mine, and I didn't want him to be. He embodied every lowly part of me. Every mistake I'd ever made and the shameful situation I found myself in. He meant loneliness. He meant captivity. He meant the loss of any future relationship. Any future respect. Any future. He was the symbol that I had ultimately failed in life. He strangled me. He suffocated me. He was, in essence, the end of my life, my hopes and my dreams. And myself.

Despite all that was happening, I had somehow miraculously managed to complete my degree and graduated in my second trimester. Writing my dissertation whilst fat, pregnant and unpacking the house I had moved into. Having left my life in London behind for new horizons.

Or so I thought. By the time my son was six months old I had shamefacedly returned to live at home with my mother and fatally returned to the horror that was my relationship. With him and with her.

I spent the next three years of my life being mocked, shamed and pushed around. I tried to leave. Many times. And I did. Briefly. But to what? To where? To whom? I had no one. So round and round we went in our abusive cycle of sorrys and beatings. I was broken mentally, but still working. In a position where I judged others for the same shame. Constantly living in fear that I would be found out for the charlatan I was. For the hypocrisy of my position. Confiding in a mother who was complicit in my shame and consistently being disowned by a father who couldn't bear me being controlled by a man other than him.

It was a friend at work who finally saved me. Craftily suggesting I make a record with the police. 'Just in case'. It was the voice notes that got him in the end. The arrogance in declaring his ability to do to me as he pleased. The hilarity of him referring to himself in the third person. Like the all-powerful god he saw himself as. And the threat to break my face off the curb. *American History X* style.

The police and the Magistrates' Court were astounded at his ego. His conviction in the fact that he said stuff like that to me all the time, so knew I wasn't *really* scared for my life. And it was the bail conditions that finally allowed me time to breathe. Time to reassess. Space to move forward with my life. To find some strength and conviction of my own.

Still. By the time he was looking at seven years at a Crown Court, he was back. Wooing me with promises of the family I had never had. For myself or for my children. And I was wavering. Did I really want my son to have no father? he asked. Did I really want to be the one responsible for my child's loss? he goaded. How could I ever live with myself? he pressed. So, like the fool I was, I pleaded with the court not to incarcerate him.

Still, I dreamt of Courtney. In my dreams he was so close I could feel him. Smell him. Sense him. His unconscious presence was more real than the faded memories I had of his touch, his words. His love. And I often longed for him.

One morning I woke with a start. Recalling Courtney's untimely death in my dream. I consoled myself by checking his presence on social media, comforted knowing that he was very much alive and apparently happy in a new relationship. That stung. I couldn't help myself, so I messaged him. A perfunctory message of warning to look out for rogue bus drivers and be safe on the roads. My heart sank at the lack of acknowledgement. Maybe it had all been in my head. Maybe he had never loved me. Maybe all those tortured glances I saw and the feeling of home that I had felt in his arms was nothing but a self-indulgent fantasy.

Two years later. Six years after our goodbye and the day after my son's father was let off with a warning and a five-year restraining order, Courtney came back into my life. He was only just seeing this message, he wrote. He couldn't believe he was actually looking at my face, he wrote. He missed me, he wrote. He wanted to see me. My heart swelled at the kindness in his message. The openness. His words thumped against my chest, and I was overwhelmed with happiness at the remote possibility that he might just care.

So, we began talking. Sending messages back and forth, falling back into the tergiversate rhythm of our past. Hearing what was unsaid and feeling what was never expressed. We spoke on Christmas Day, Courtney concerned that I was all alone, my kids spending their first ever Christmas away from me. And my heart swelled. He called me drunk, professing his love. Asking for him to be the only one I relied on, the one I wanted. The one I needed. And my heart swelled. He spent hours convincing me of my worth, of my power and of his unwavering presence in my life. And my heart swelled.

When we finally met, the fireworks that had been packed back into their box for a more suitable celebration, the electricity turned off for fear of burning out and the deafening thump of my heart, so long suppressed in light of the pain it had endured, all returned in an instant. The room permeated with lust and fire and longing. Still. All remained unsaid. All remained unexpressed. All remained a delicate dance around our own and each other's fragile hearts and egos. There was no denying it though. It was all still there. In reams. In droves.

In love.

And it *was* all the same. Even down to the new 'real' girlfriend. The new serious relationship. The new unspoken attraction. My new role as the side hustle. So, naturally, I fell back into character. Unable and unaware of how to be loved, how to command respect and how to let go of the absolute need to mean something. Again becoming relationship therapist to the man I wanted.

But this time, I quietly bided my time and my lip. Because I was not completely debilitated. I was now a *woman*, after all, and if I had learnt nothing else in our time apart, I knew that being a shoulder to cry on and a trusted advisor has its advantages. It is also, ladies, to your advantage to express your decision to allow the person you love to move forward in their life. Lovingly. Encouragingly. And, furthermore, to respectfully request that they stop engaging in any loving exchanges with you. Thus, leaving them disarmed.

It had been six years after all, and I was not going to be put into a box and kept there for anyone's amusement. No matter how real their loved seemed. So, I manipulated a stake hold in him. I made myself desirable. Indispensable. And completely unobtainable in a completely obtainable way. Within two months he was living in my house. As a 'friend', of course. And I was revelling in my undeniable cleverness.

But the thing is, anything that's built on sand is sure to crumble and collapse. Anything built on deception and lies, infidelity and purposeful pain to others can only beget more of the same. As a thing can only develop into more of what it already is.

I'm sorry to his girlfriend. I knew what I was doing, and I did it anyway. To prove myself. To prove my worth. To finally be The One. The one above all else. To compete in some illegitimate love triangle between me, Courtney and my old self. The old self that was never quite good enough. Never quite sure. Never quite real to him. So I snared him, and I brought him into my home in a frenzy of lustful whim. Into my children's lives and into my bed.

It's funny because even though I had orchestrated the whole thing, forcing the relationship in hushed, stealthy manipulation, it was still real. The feelings were real, the care was real, the love between us was real. Undoubtably. And moreover, what was still abundantly real was my complete, absolute, unavoidable inability to feel worthy, myself, or 'the one'.

I was still completely powerless. To him. To relationships. To men. Muted objections filled my lips but never uttered breath. Muted screams filled my head. I spent my days detesting all his pig-headed, arrogant ways, and I spent my nights hating myself for never saying no. For wanting his touch and his lust. For giving my body and my soul to him even though I knew. For feeling it was the only power I had over him. And knowing it was his ultimate power over me.

We lived like that for months. In love. And lust. And hate. And fear. And power. And powerlessness.

It was amazing though! Whole weekends of partying. New friends. Tenderness. Conspiracy theories. Mind-blowing sex. Festivals. Action films. Copious drugs of all sorts. Holding hands on the street. Black Power debates. Arguing. Making up. Getting drunk. Dinner at the dinner table at six. Work in the morning. Holding each other close at night. Dancing our arses off. Finding my home in the dip of his neck. Making love and fighting wars.

I never knew until then just how lonely I had been. I never knew until then that Courtney was my best friend. I never knew until then just how little I knew about being in a relationship and just how ill-equipped I was for it. Perhaps I still didn't know it then because I was never able to share my feelings or let anything go. I was never able to communicate. In any way. About anything. I was never able to stop myself retracting all my love and withdrawing myself and my fragile little heart into the cavity inside myself, built just for this purpose in a time long forgotten.

He was no better though. Raging from abandonment and mummy issues. Womanising all his life and knowing no better way to self-medicate and redress the balance every time I was holed up in my cave of misery, shrouded in self-pity and self-indulgence.

I knew. Every time he was unfaithful, I knew. Like a cheater's Spidey-sense buzzing uncontrollably in my fingers and my ears, and my gut twisted and turned with bitterness and rage, and my heart slowly started to beat more quietly, exhausted and fatigued from the effort being in pain brought.

And I forgave him. At each juncture. Because I truly understood him. I knew his past and the pain he had endured and been witness to before he was old enough to know his own mind or how thick his skin had grown. And how hardened his sweet, sweet heart had become. And I knew that it was still there underneath, strangled by anguish, still trying to beat. Trying to breathe.

I knew how damaging it was to watch your mum, your *mum*, fall into the depths of crack addiction. To have to pull her out of crack dens at the age of fifteen. And watch her prostitute herself. And know that everybody knew. I knew the shame and the embarrassment and the seething rage it caused him. The tears that he would never let fall. And how broken his heart was. I knew the fury he felt, feeling responsible for a woman that everyone else had abandoned, and only because everyone else had abandoned her. Even though she had abandoned him.

And I knew how alone he had been in all of it. Missing school and his GCSEs to care for a sister everyone had forgotten. And how it was he who was invariably forgotten in the process. I know how he turned to crime to pay for food and how there was nothing in the house but wine and weed. Purchased for his dad's obligatory release upon his triumphant return from work. A job that never seemed to keep the lights on. Or put food in the fridge. But where was *his* release? In women, I guess. In loving and hating and owning and claiming them. And through it, reclaiming himself and the powerlessness of his situation.

And I knew that his only comfort throughout all of this was staring up at the night sky. Silently scared and quietly resolute. Searching the heavens for his constellation. The one that had become his only source of light when all the lights at home were out. His beacon in hard times. *His* guiding star.

And I knew now that his only comfort was me. All the good and the bad and the ugly I represented to him. His very own slice of home. Even if he didn't know how to love me right.

So the first time I caught him I went through the motions of being devasted. Even though it was just my pride that was hurt. Really, I knew he was just harmlessly talking to girls, but my ego couldn't stomach being second best to any other female. So I took my anger out on his clothes and the necklace he had bought me. The only piece of jewellery he had ever given to a girl. I threw him out and took him back in a day. By the evening we were making love and I was counselling him again about his need to be loved and accepted, about the everlasting impact of his mother's departure, and about the concept of emotional cheating. Guiding him on how my power and my dignity had been given into the hands of another, without my express permission. All concepts he had never before considered, but accepted from me because he knew that, ultimately, I loved him. That ultimately, I was his best friend.

The second time was more painful. Because the relationship was more serious. Because he knew me more. My fears, my worries and my needs as a broken person. He understood and accepted how vulnerable I was and the intrinsic link for me between self-worth and this relationship. The constant competition I was in, between me and everyone else. And because *I* was the real girlfriend this time. It wasn't fair to place him as the centre of my universe, but he knew it. And he accepted that burden. Even so, he couldn't help but seek instant gratification in times of difficulty, in times of rejection. Like a recovering addict relapsing when the going got rough. I wonder where he might have seen that before.

My cousin alerted me to it. An accidental like on Instagram. Easily done, I guess. When you're stalking someone's page. This time I decided to take action, and I reached out to her. She, of course, thought they were embarking on a future together and that I was old news. And we spoke and concocted a plan while he lay upstairs in my bed. And laughed as we exchanged messages back and forth, her screenshotting his deception in real time to my horror and amusement.

When I finally went upstairs to confront him. I was confronted. With the "what the fuck was I talking about?" gambit. He was hurt, angry, disgusted by my accusations. He was outraged at my heinous suggestion that he could be so calculating. So cold. That he was still that guy. How dare I?

So I called her.

Right in front of him.

And smugly watched as the colour drained from his face. I was fierce. I was powerful. I was indestructible. Oh, what fun it was to finally catch him in the act. Except it wasn't really fun. My relationship was in tatters and my heart and head were cracking open. But I was drunk. Drunk on the power of it all. Revelling in my own self-importance. How clever and wily I was. How cunning and artful I had become.

He didn't have time for all these games. I was a fool, a loser and a wannabe. A desperate little girl who should be ashamed of my actions.

So I smoked more weed and somehow ended up the one passed out on the doghouse sofa.

The following day me and this girl arranged to meet. With his ex-girl, the girl I stole him from, to boot. We all got dressed up. And drunk. And high. And man bashed him. His scrawny frame. His dodgy hairline. His stupid alien ears. The piece of food that always got stuck in the corner of his mouth when he ate. And I delighted in the fact that I was the one, the only one, he had ever bought anything for. The only one he had ever begged back. The only one he had ever loved? It shouldn't have, but it gave me reassurance and fed me hope and importance in my hunger for glorification.

I returned home to him begging me back through the letterbox. And just like that the frenzy was over. The anger had all been spewed out the night before, and I was subsiding. Quietly celebrating my victory. But not against him. Against all the other girls who paled in comparison to me. Against my old self who'd had and known nothing of this type of triumph, this conquest over him.

It's a strange paradigm to feel powerful and worthless at the same time. To want to be wanted, but only in comparison to everyone else. I knew it then, even if I would never admit it. I had become addicted to the chase and to the game of it all. And I hated and loved him for it. And I hated and hated myself.

Something shifted for me after that day. We went through the motions, but it felt like something inside of me had changed. We went out, but

I was never comfortable. We watched films, but I was never able to concentrate. We made love, but it felt alien to me.

My heart was not in recovery.

It was comatose.

And I stayed because I had no strength to leave. I didn't want to find the strength to leave. Where else would I get my assurances? I opened my legs because I didn't know how to say no. And I closed my mouth because I didn't know how to speak my mind. Too scared that it might mean what I knew it meant. That I was unhappy and falling out of love. So I retreated more and more into my cavern. Finding more and more fault in him and taking back any love, affection or care that I once gave freely. And he knew it. But just like every other meaningful conversation between us, the silence of our predicament held silently in the ever-expanding void.

I was again lying silently back.

But this time, it was I who was the perpetrator. I was the figure on top of me, goading me to fight back. *If I was strong enough.*

Before the third and final time, the relationship was now a horrific mess of pain, suffering, resentment, hurt and anger. We hated and loved one another in equal measure, and the dysfunction of it all was both exhausting and exciting. We used drugs more and more to escape the torment of our predicament, the pain of living with and losing each other. He had no time for the drama of me, and I had no patience anymore. For my position as his maid. For his position as man of the house. Despite owning no house, contributing no funds and being far from a man. I was tired and lonely. And all the problems we had always had were amplified by my disgust of him and myself.

I often thought about everything he had done. I had a constant monologue in my head, reminding me of how little he cared, of how worthless I was, of how humiliated I felt. And of just whose fault it all was. I could spend hours staring into the hole in my chest, filled with bitterness and hatred. Listening, and being overcome by the voices. The voices that had always been there to remind me of just how little I meant. Only now they were right. They had evidence, with their PowerPoint presentations and flip charts. They played me reruns of my most glorious and most recent pathetic encounters. And I sat on and watched. Wide-eyed and mummified. Helplessly settling for what could only be but the truth:

I deserved it.

I was useless and worthless.

I was nothing and no one.

I was unlovable and nobody cared.

And where was God?

I didn't even ask.

I had succumbed to the voices.

On other days I fought back. But not against the voices. Or the feeling of ever-simmering rot in my stomach. But against Courtney. I fought back with scathing comments. And in looks of disappointment. And in passive aggression. All mastered throughout my childhood. I made him feel as worthless as I was. Silently. Shrewdly. Deviously. And he plunged into as much pain and despair as me, until we were both drowning in it. Choking and spluttering on the unexpressed shame we both felt. Until eventually there was nothing left but violence and cruelty. Disdain and distance.

It was the eve of my thirty-third birthday, and as usual we were arguing. He was a let-down. I was a cold-hearted bitch. He left and didn't come home. So I woke and I went to work. With my head held high and my stomach sinking low. He messaged me telling me how much he loved me and how sad, disappointed and confused he was. I ignored him.

After that night it was like freefall. Gravity pulling us to our impending death on the tarmac. We barely spoke. We barely touched. We were strangers to one another. Strangers who got high and fucked. It was all we had left. It went on like that for just over a month, with the relationship teetering on a precipice. A cliff we were both too scared to jump off, despite us both already plummeting rapidly to the ground.

26 August 2016, and I woke in my eldest son's room, having slept there due to the Courtney passed out on top of me. Him getting so drunk the night before he couldn't walk, bullying me in front my friend and walking out of the house declaring it was over, me having refused to kiss his pungent-smelling lips.

So, given he was incapacitated, I took his phone and his thumb and helped myself to the truth. What I found was heartbreaking. Him and a girl. On film. On the eve of my birthday. Getting dressed again. And laughing. Carelessly laughing. At me, no doubt. At my humiliation. At my life. And my love.

I was incensed.

I was enraged.

And by the time I woke him, I was crazed with bitterness and fury. 'You need to leave by the time I get home', I said to his drunken, bewildered face. 'I don't care where you go. Maybe to her house. In New Cross. Pepe's Estate, if I'm not mistaken.' He was drunk and confused and infuriated. So I called the police. And he threw all my clothes into the garden. Hangers and all.

After he had been peacefully removed, I silently dressed for the festival I was attending and proceeded to get drunk on the journey. He called me. I ignored him. I called him back, and he asked me to whom he was speaking. I fell about in manic hysterics. Altogether it was a good time. We partied and we afterpartied. I met my primary school friend who I hadn't seen in years. She got us into the VIP box, and we watched on as she got removed for selling us ecstasy. We took it and forgot all about her.

When I woke in the morning, he was outside calling me. You can't come in, I told him. I'm indisposed. Wasn't it fun hearing him squirm at the thought of my legs wide open and wrapped around another? How clever and wily I was. How cunning and artful I had become.

He cried in front of me on the sofa. I sat monotone opposite him. Straight-backed and straight-faced. My heart secretly summersaulting in my chest at how broken he was. And for me! It was often an image

I would return to, get my juices going. It was such a turn-on. A man that no one could pin down crying and broken for me. Pleading for me. Longing for me. I had won. I lifted my trophy in a blaze of glory and supercilious arrogance. 9.7 on the scoreboard and a victory lap for good measure.

But the momentum of anger and fury only lasts so long, and my victory lap slowly turned into relapse. So I went alone to the holiday booked for our family in quiet shame. My rage simmering and the pain beginning to brew. Beginning to stew.

My heart was no longer comatose.

It was flatlined.

And the rot in my stomach churned.

And the voices in my head screamed out at me in cruel and righteous triumph. For the victory was theirs and theirs alone.

And where was God?

Who cared anymore.

I returned to a contrite and concerned Courtney, and by the second day my legs were open for him again. But my heart and soul were missing. Fallen out of me. Lost somewhere in the wilderness of the past. I cried and beat him every time I gave myself to him, and he held me in dutiful sorrow. I was broken. I was wounded. I was returning from the battle, pieces of me missing. A dishonourable discharge. Because I was dishonourable.

Something changed inside me after those days. I was weighted down. I was sunken. I lived under and inside a cloud. Darkness weighing heavy on me like an invisible blanket of depression, obscured from the world and seen and felt by only me. I woke every morning tired. From the pain. From the emptiness. From the sorrow and the grief I felt coursing through my veins. It was like being electrified with hurt. Or slowly electrocuted with it. Tender from the pain of it all. Like a constant buzzing. Visceral. Lifeless but alive. Alive with something dead inside. Unnatural and disgusting.

I lived in that sunken place while Courtney still partied. Running away for days at a time. I had no patience or care for him anymore, but I couldn't find it in me to leave. Within a month I was pregnant. Again. It was like carrying a carcass. Death infecting my body. Slowly and deliberately diseasing me from the inside out. Courtney left me to deal with things myself, opting for the familiar comfort of a drunken, drug-fuelled escape. And I dreamed of our unborn baby, my mother's long overdue acceptance and the love this would foster between us all.

After the abortion I finally fell into the abyss, drunken and desperate for him to acknowledge my grief, but finding nothing but distance and disdain. He was as broken as me and in no position to mend anything. I thought a lot about death, surmising it probably didn't feel much different from the sunken place I inhabited. There was nothing alive in me anyway. Not anymore. Not now.

Courtney didn't believe me. He scoffed at my cries of wolf and admonished me. Until he found me one day sat in my car. Face down. Hair matted. Lifeless and limp. Dying in front of his eyes. The light in my eyes where my soul used to be burnt out and my chest hollow and empty. We took me to the doctors after that. Citalopram. 20mg. That would sort me out. And to be fair, it did. I could raise my head in the morning. Look at something other than the floor. Brush my teeth. Speak to my children. But the rot remained and the voices heckled and jeered. It was constant. There was no escaping it. So I smiled. A crazed and wild smile and hoped that nobody could tell I was fallen into madness. I denied all suggestion that I was unwell and danced and played with my children in a manner bordering on hysteria. And the rot remained and the voices heckled and jeered.

By February 2017 I had discarded the medication and we were in Tobago. What a beautiful setting to hate a loved one. Courtney was now more committed and as a result dying inside from my lack of interest or care. He looked at me in quiet longing again, and I looked to the ceiling while we made love. Lying silently back. And listened to the voices. They were now my only counsel. My only friends. I moaned on cue and forced climax to allow the torture to be over. I couldn't stand him and he knew it. But as always it remained unsaid. I danced and flirted with strangers in front of him and belittled him whenever the opportunity presented.

But despite this, nothing made me feel better. Yet, regaling myself with stories of my humiliation, his desperation and my hatred for him were beautifully indulgent fantasies. I clung to them like life itself. I thirsted for them like water in the desert. They were my mirage. My home. My comfort. I was consumed with pain, bitterness and rage. But my exhumed body was nothing more than passively wrathful.

We argued. We watched films. We danced. We ate dinner at the dinner table at six. We played with the kids. We held hands on the street. We worked. We partied. We took copious amounts of drugs. We forgot and relived our pain. We made love and war. And I watched it all. From the sunken place. Me and the voices. My only allies. My antagonists. My existence now.

Nothing was the same.

I wasn't the same.

I was inhabited by a presence of hatred that was all-consuming.

Rotting me from the inside out.

And who the *fuck* is God?

And who the *fuck* cares.

I'd now graduated to sertraline. 20mg. It was ineffective. So I weaned myself off of it. Over the course of a day. Nothing was working. So we did what any other self-respecting couple on the verge of collapse would do. We moved 220 miles away together. To start afresh. It was that or have a baby, and I'm pretty sure I was rightly barren.

July 2018 and we were living in Liverpool. Why? Because that was where the party was at. We were desperately unhappy. Knowing nothing other than each other and the inter-dependent relationship we now championed.

Courtney, by now, was sick of my disregard for him. My quiet contempt. And my eyes were red rimmed, bloodshot. Nearly demented and filled with something else, someone else. I barely recognised myself, and I was tortured at the knowledge that I was not who I was anymore. But I couldn't stop. I couldn't cease. I couldn't see. I was a woman possessed. I was charged, electrified with loathing. Preoccupied with nothing but my pain and my distrust and my hatred. Pure, unadulterated, all-consuming, uncontrollable hate. All packaged in a perfectly controlled body.

The feeling of being worthless was familiar. The knowledge that nobody, not even God, cared or thought about me was long certified in my head and my heart. And the feeling of being a fraud and a charlatan was not new to me. Except now I didn't even recognise the person staring back at me, the thoughts in my head or the words in my mouth. I was distorted. Like the mirrors at an unfun house. My face and my soul stretched and thinned until they were unnatural and monstrous. I was the monster. I was evil. I dreamt evil. I thought evil. I whispered evil under my breath, and I felt it deep, deep down in my soul. I was the damned walking the earth. Playing at goodness, kindness and empathy. Like a clown, a joker. A fool. I lived in my costume, the only person aware of the true extent of my iniquity.

It would spill out of Courtney every so often. His mouth needing to expel the bile in his stomach for me. 'You're a parasite. A witch. A bitch. You're vile and you disgust me', he would spit. And I would cry because I knew it was true. And I would cry because I knew it would make him feel guilty. And I would cry because I knew I would get the attention and the comfort I so desperately needed.

He started uni, although he never went. He partied and drank and stayed up all night and spent all our money and blamed me for his unhappiness and used his newfound role as 'stepdad' as an excuse for his own exhaustion and lack of care. I worked and I worked, sometimes staying away for days on end and sometimes staying up until the early hours to compensate for the money that haemorrhaged out of his bank account. Him now in control of the family. Him now the 'man of the house'. And me with no redress for the powerless state I had willingly put myself in. What did I expect? Cheating the system and trying to get ahead through lies and deception?

But no matter how much I worked we could never get ahead. Our castle was built on and out of sand. And we skulked around the grounds, manning our respective wings. Drawbridges, moats and tower walls between us. And archers at the ready. We hated one another. Me for his uncaring, selfish, childish nature. And him for my unloving, unavailable, untrusting heart.

But just like any worthy advisories, we were intrinsically linked. We were unable to live without one another. We were committed to this bitter feud. To the bitter end. It dictated our very existence and the parameters of the relationship. The parameters of ourselves. Because the thing is, as much as we were both controlled by one another's jealousy and guilt and disgrace, without it, there was a void that begged to be filled. A void that pitted itself on mine and his need to be needed. Even if it was chronically toxic and undeniably corrosive.

Because ultimately, we still cared. Or maybe because Courtney had finally committed himself to one woman and couldn't turn back now.

Or maybe because we still loved each other, he searched for alternative therapies for me, and I tried to dial down the voices and swallow the rot so I could be a more loving girlfriend. We had stints of happiness and connection, but they were always interrupted by my vicious nature. By the unnatural entity that governed my thoughts and my words and my heart. I felt disgusted by his touch and found myself, as usual, lying back silently, waiting for it to be over. Disgusted in myself and repulsed by him. Courtney systematically relapsed into drugs and alcohol to cope. I didn't care. Even though I could see him dying before my eyes, the light of his spirit flickering and fading behind his. And the pain I felt for us blackened my vision and my world.

It had to end. There was no denying it. Despite Courtney's constant denial. Despite his need to hold onto the only woman he had given any part of his heart to other than his forsaking mother. Despite his incessant need to be right. To prove himself to himself. To prove that he could be loved if he allowed himself to be. To prove he hadn't given himself in vain. It had to end.

But through his stubbornness, and his need to not be forsaken again, he had become my guru, my counsel, my inspiration. He never gave up. He couldn't give up. And pep talks and reassurances about our commitment and our power as a couple became like a drug to me. I was addicted to his belief, his faith, his vision. I needed it. I engineered my behaviour and our lives to be renewed in his faith in me and in us. It was intoxicating to be needed so much. To be pleaded for. I was the deity, the muse, the worshipped. I was his false god, and I revelled in his pain and torture just so I could feast on his devotion to me.

I was never devoted though. To him, to me, to our family, our life. To God. I was devoted to consuming him, feeding off of him like the parasite he invariably knew I was. Sometimes I feigned affection. Sometimes I offered compassion, kind words, motivation. But even as I did, I looked on at myself, revelling in my own beautiful mercy. My own glorious grace. Basking in the kindness of a benevolent queen.

It was all a game. But not the sophisticated dance of chess, more like sport of the queen's hunt – if animals could talk and plead for your compassion. It was fun and exciting. Arguing and living in fear and hating and fucking. I got off on the crazy. I *was* the crazy. I was crazed and manic in my rule. The tyrant dictator of his world. Inevitably constructing my own downfall. My kingdom delighted in fornication and sexuality. I controlled my loyal subject through my body and my open legs. Luring and trapping him. Needing to be desired. Never wanting to be possessed but never being able to say no.

And this is where I lived. This was the world I created and occupied, haunted by the ghost of my own immorality. Empowered by the hold of what lay in between my legs and appalled at what I had become. Tortured by the abhorrent way I needed to be needed. And he was no better. Seeking out gratification and comfort through the admiration of all women. Using his penis to occupy and dominate. Only us both finding that it was we who were dominated. We who were overtaken. We who were governed and not the governors. No wonder God had introduced us. No wonder God had forsaken us.

When it finally ended, we were both exhausted. I left him in a flurry of indignation. Him having disrespected me for the last time, abandoned me for the last time, spent the last of my money, taken the last of his drugs. Nevertheless, we made empty promises of a future. We promised ourselves and each other that we would find a way back and would be true and devoted even in our separation. So it came as an earth-shattering revelation when he told me he had met someone else. One week after we separated. And for the two months we had inhabited the same house and often, the same bed.

I was undone. I was broken. I was empty. 'We knew he would do this', they spat. 'We knew he was disloyal and faithless', they declared. 'We knew you were never the one. Second to all else. You deserve it. Bow down, we earnt it!' And they goaded and sniggered. Mocked and sneered. Pointed at me and to me and for me in disgust.

I spent just over two weeks in grief and mourning until finding some comfort and liberation in the realisation of my own role in my relationship. I attended a conference for people stuck in themselves. A cognitive-behavioural-type gig. It was helpful. For the moment. And I wrote to him about all my rackets. About all the things I pretended I didn't want but actively facilitated, complied with, compelled. About my persecution of him throughout our relationship and my active denigration of him to our friends. It was the first time I had taken responsibility for anything, and he was aghast. Invariably, we reconnected. He had slept with someone else, and I was dating. It enraged and excited us. We needed that reassurance. The reassurance we found in only one another. We made more promises. To be different. To love, to care, to talk. Within a few weeks we were arguing. I was back in my sunken hole, all my renewed faith and practices strewn aside. I hated to love him, and once again he was grandiosely burdened with my brokenness.

Except this time, Courtney *was* renewed in his commitment to me, having made the decision to remove himself from the noxious equation of our relationship, and was supporting me dutifully throughout. He kept his promises to me. He manned the house and manned up. He cared for and guided and loved my children like a true father. He was steadfast, immovable in his promise to me and this relationship. Even though it was clearly sucking the life out of him. He exhausted himself in servitude to me. He poured everything from his cup into me and stayed and stayed when a better man would have run for his life. Even though I was menacing in my looks and my deeds and my love. Even though he had no room for himself or his own needs and even though I fell so deep into a depression that I couldn't be shaken into a response.

And why did we do it to ourselves? Beside our vile needs, our shameful vanity and our persistent self-loathing? Because, I suppose, when it comes down to it, we are rooted to one another. there is an enduring quality about this person in my life. Something that gives us hope and strength in dark times and something that causes us to love beyond all reason. He is rooted to me. He is etched on my heart and imprinted on my soul. He is branded to me. And I to him. God *did* put him here for me. To destroy and be destroyed by. To love and cherish and demolish and scar. To learn by and from. And to ultimately change me. At my very core. In my very soul. To facilitate and be witness to my salvation. My miracle. As without him I would still be lost. In the sunken place. Tortured and bound by an enemy that I didn't know I needed to fear.

It's funny, though, because even though we didn't know it, we did. We knew the crack. The story. The enemy. The Good News. But it was only through Courtney finally offering me what he knew I always needed. Openly. Honestly. Righteously. That I was finally confronted with the truth. The stark reality that it was indeed just me who held the rot. That the rot lived within me. Was nourished by me and crept out, perennially strangling all around me like a vine-twisted hand of poisonous ivy, choking the life out of me and anything that loved me.

Except I thought the rot *was* me. That it was me who was not worthy. Me undeserved. Me unlovable and unable to love.

And it was with that erroneous thought that it was decided.

I had to go.

I had to die.

And there.

Finally.

As He always had been.

There was God.

22 June 2020

I*t's not me. It's not me. It's not me.*

Forget all about the torture plagued upon me during the day. The anger. The jealousy. The greed. The flashes of hate on a continuum. And the never-relenting, all-consuming, heart-breaking feeling of loss. Forget about the loss of love. Loss of friendship. Loss of confidence. Loss of kindness. The feeling of always being on the outside. Of everything and everyone. Forget about knowing that no matter what you did, said, were, weren't, could or couldn't be, you would always be wretched. You would always be worthless. You would never amount to anything. But more importantly, forget that God, in all His wisdom, in all His mercy, in all His love, would never, ever love you.

Oh, the torment. The unwavering pain and the exhaustion. And it is *exhausting. To believe you are rejected by the One you never knew loved you so much. Forget about all that.*

It's the nights. The nights were the worst. Depicting images immoral enough to disgust you. To send shivers down your spine. To send you into madness. I dreamt so many things. I cheated on Courtney multiple times. Happily, gratefully raped by countless faceless men. Over and over. I smashed babies' heads in. I sexually assaulted children. Sometimes dreaming of orgasm, but always stirring confused. Waking to find my heels and my ears imprinted in the mattress, pressed down by some unknown entity. Disgusted and guilty. And a distinct hate for myself. Questioning with a desperation bordering on insanity if this was me. Deep down. In the depths. If my heart was indeed iniquity personified. If my daytime face was nothing but a pure masquerade. A façade. If I was the fraud I always felt I was. And it weighed heavy on my heart every waking moment. Like an anchor chained to hell. To the place I felt I belonged. Confirming what I already knew about myself. That I was evil. That I was unlovable. That I was rejected. And underserved.

Note to self: That's the game. That's their one and only purpose. To take your soul from you. To trap you within yourself. To convince you that you are lowly, repulsive, monstrous, wicked, abhorrent. Something that God would never love, never forgive, never save.

Funny thing is. Once you realise what you knew all along. This thing. This thing that sent you over the edge. This thing that feasted on your darkness and anguish. This thing that revelled in your delirium. This thing that celebrated your hysteria.

That. It's. Not. You.
You're free.
And it's not me. It's not me. It's not me.
And I am.
Free.

What if, Two

WHAT IF, 2) **IT DIDN'T TAKE AN EXORCISM TO WAKE YOU UP? IF YOUR PARENTS, YOUR PARENTING, YOUR CHILDHOOD AND YOUR ANCESTORS WEREN'T THE CAUSE OF YOUR SELF-PERPETUATING LOATHING? WHAT IF POP-PSYCHOLOGY WASN'T THE ONLY PLAUSIBLE THEORY TO EXPLAIN THE ORIGINS OF EVERY DESPICABLE, DEGRADING, DEVIANT THOUGHT YOU HAD?**

WHAT IF YOU DREW BACK THE VEIL TO REVEAL THAT GOOD AND EVIL ACTUALLY EXISTED?
WHAT IF YOU WOKE UP AND REALISED WHO'S SIDE YOUR IGNORANCE HAD CHOSEN FOR YOU?

WOULD YOU CHOOSE AGAIN?

I never knew I had a social worker. She came to see me when my parents were getting divorced. Imagine an age where social workers helped you through something as menial as that. Funny they weren't there for the rest of it. Apparently I had blocked this out because I hadn't even heard of one until I read about it in the college prospectus. Did I want to help others? Yes. Did I have a keen interest in psychology? Yes. Was helping the next generation important to me? Certainly. Well, apparently, social work was for me.

I was twenty and a new mother. Joshua. My miracle. My saving grace. My reality check. I can remember tentatively placing my fingers through the hole of his ventilation pod. Just after the doctors had told me he would never walk, or talk, or sit up, or feed himself. That his brain was too severely damaged. Just after my mother had asked if my weed consumption had caused it and stared at me with palpable blame and unabated shame, despite being assured I wasn't the culprit. Him, no bigger than a bag of sugar, prem nappies covering his entire torso, and sprouting hair everywhere. And me, filled to the brim with indescribable love, from the tips of my toes to the depths of my heart. Love in my gut, in my very being. In the fingers that tentatively reached out to him. Thinking to myself, how could anyone forsake their own child? How could anyone take something so precious, a gift to you, from you, and make it hurt? Reject it. Scorn it. Fail it. I remember whispering into his tiny ear, "I'll never hurt you. I'll never do to you what was done to me. I will always love you. You are mine, but you are also your own. And I celebrate and treasure you." Looking back now, I kind of hope the Perspex muffled my voice and muted my hasty declarations.

Maybe it was the baby brain that made me want to go back to college. Maybe it was the loneliness. Maybe it was the lure of free childcare. Maybe it was the mind-numbing daily routine of monotony that was about to cause me to engulf my own child. Like a man, island bound, stranded and ravenous with crazed isolation. Staring at his starved and skeletal accomplice with greedy lips. Maybe it was my mother's admonition ringing in my ears about the need to get a 'real job'. The need. Not the want. Maybe it was the necessity of fulfilling the solemn role of parent. The ridiculousness that it was me who was doing it and the stark reminder that, ultimately, I was just playing. Playing at home. A game that had never appealed to me as a child. Being too selfish and wrapped up in my own existence and my own crisis to ever want to have to give to another. I used to say I was too selfish to have a baby. I liked buying shoes. And sleeping. And lounging about. And smoking weed. But the truth was, I was just scared. I never wanted the responsibility of trying to care for something in a way that was alien to me. Of giving something to someone else that I had no idea how to give. That I didn't have to give.

But here I found myself. Filling out my admission form and putting my best foot forward. Turns out social work suited me. I was intelligent and bright, a quick learner and good with the clever words. I understood people. I got the theory, and I was praised in my practice. By the time I started my first job, I was already up and coming. Apparently, my reputation preceded me. And to be honest, I liked it. I had a penchant for uncovering people, for understanding their needs. And their weaknesses. And for explaining why their child was at risk in a way that was accessible, acceptable and mostly, human.

But mainly I loved the kids. I felt them. I saw them, and I began to advocate for what *I* had recognised as a child. That if you can find a way to communicate, if you can find a way to listen, if you can really respect and appreciate them, even the smallest child has something to say. And moreover, something to teach us. They get it. So much easier and quicker and realer than we ever do.

I saw myself in their lost faces. In their confusion. In their silence and in their cries. And in every time they were overlooked in the face of budget, or parental justice, or the morality of sustaining families, or our own clever, self-important hypotheses.

I remembered. All too clearly the absurdity, the confusion of your parent being the perp. The lack of understanding by the complex and oh-so superior adult mind of just how damaging it all was in its simplicity. And imagined, easily, the likely feeling of perplexity when faced with the arrogance of all the adults around you championing their own causes through you. Somehow reliving and resolving their own childhood trauma through your own. And it broke my heart and spurred me on.

But to what? Wasn't I doing the same? Wasn't I reliving and resolving my own trauma? Wasn't my need to fight for the rights of all children just a façade for my own childhood powerlessness? Maybe it was better I had never had a social worker – in those times of real need. I wouldn't have wanted to learn so early that even the system is corrupt. Even the system is complicit in your abuse. Because ultimately it is the people, albeit meaningful and well intentioned in their plights, who make it. And people are flawed. People are blind to themselves. People are dangerous.

I often think about why I was so good at my job. I used to think it was my tenacity for the truth, my attention to the detail of each person's psyche and my ability to positively manipulate. Positive bullying, I call it now. I used to think it was my love of children and my desire to champion their needs. I used to think it was because I was so good at connection, with and to them. Because I really was. I am. I love to be able to meet a child where they're at. Child-led and child-focussed, we call it in the biz. But perhaps it was what drove me that needed a little more deliberation.

I was bullied prolifically in primary school. I had next to no friends. Save for the new ones. Before they upgraded to their real friends or went back to their home countries. It wasn't so much that I was jeered at, or pushed around, or called bad names, or told, "You can't sit with us". I was just ignored. Which in a lot of ways is worse. Being invisible isn't a superpower. You don't get to hide in plain sight and skulk out your enemies or find out dirty secrets. Or play pranks on people who love you anyway, in a fun-filled, PG-13, family-friendly, jester kind of way. In real life, you are plainly *in* sight. You're just ignored.

I can remember walking the playgrounds at school, eyes in my back like sunburn. Some gleeful and some contrite in the knowledge that I was alone, and nobody wanted to play with me. It wasn't anybody's fault I suppose. I started late in the year and spent most of my time with my older brother's friends. Much to his delight.

Phia Eastown hated me at first glance. For reasons I wouldn't understand until I was much older and most women hated me at first glance. A role that I would eventually succumb to and ultimately revel in. So I wasn't allowed to play with any of her friends. And everyone was her friend. Thus, I walked round and round the playground and around and around in my mind trying to appear in both places as if having no friends was a choice. A preference. I don't think I was convincing in either setting.

By the time I got to secondary school I was quietly seething and outwardly tolerant. No one at home helped. It wasn't even acknowledged that I, a mere child, had issues. That I had psychological needs that weren't being met. That I had no one to speak to about my experiences and was lost trying to figure it all out, trying to reconcile what it all meant to me and what I meant in all of it. So somewhere in my confusion I made the decision that having no friends didn't mean anything. And meant everything.

So I reinvented myself. In my secondary school years I became a beacon of sultry attitude. I allowed all the rumours about me to run rampant. Yep. Of course I had had sex already. I was so mature and cool and worldly. I was, in fact, a virgin until the age of sixteen., but it gave me notoriety, and I was finally acknowledged and recognised for something. Everyone knew who I was, and I unhappily accepted the desperate approval that this bogus acclamation and these phoney friendships gave.

But I still had no one. Not really. No one to really talk to, to really share myself with. To really be understood by or understand. No connection with the outside world, or anyone at home. Or myself. And I loved and detested it that way. I never spoke to my mum about any of it. I had learned long ago that she didn't get it. And that she didn't care to. That she just wanted me to be her own confirmation of success. And my dad was, as usual, missing in action. Both of them too wrapped up in their own childhood trauma to be able to recognise mine.

And it went on like this. All through school, through college, through uni and into every job I held thereafter. I never made any friends really. I never tried to. I was plagued with the unconscious knowledge that I couldn't sit with them. I expected rejection so rejected all relationships before they materialised.

And it was with these unearthed thoughts that I had my children. I was convinced, driven with a need to love them more than I had been. To understand them. To truly see them. As both worthy and unique. I loved my son. Even through the isolation and the upheaval. My mum had told me, in no uncertain terms, that she would not support me with my illegitimate child. And boy did she stick to it. I don't think I saw the night sky from outside of my bedroom window for at least a year and a half. Or a wise man outside my door. It was like a twilight fantasy when I finally stepped out of my house, made up and ready for a night of light-hearted debauchery. I can remember looking up at the sky in wonder and smelling the night air. Just like I used to on those long-forgotten holidays of my youth. My real youth. Before all the babies and the forsaking of my dreams.

I'm grateful for my inexperience and the arrogance of youth though. If not, I might have listened more intently when the doctors told me my son would essentially be a cabbage. But I knew no better. So I dragged him up in fortunate, blinkered ignorance. I expected no different from him than any other child of his age. Whatever that was. And I scoffed at the health visitor and my mother when they ventured concern that he wasn't walking at nearly two. Come back and talk to me if he's still shuffling around on his butt, dog-with-worms style when he's fifteen. But for now, just leave him alone.

I made a conscious decision, born of my own pain, to love him for who he was and always respect and authenticate him. No matter what my thoughts, or wants, or desires, or needs were. I managed it sometimes. I desperately wanted him to feel proud of himself and to know that he could achieve anything he wanted to. Even if it was harder for him. Even if the cookie had a slightly more crumbled brain than the other cookies. I never blamed his condition for his behaviour. I never made excuses for him. And I detested my mother every time she said he didn't understand, 'because of his poor, poor brain'. Every time she got mad when he used the term *retard*. Not to describe himself. But just because he found it funny. And seethed and laughed at the irony that it was truly only her who thought he was retarded, as she was the only one attributing this term to him.

And as a result, Joshua grew into something unrecognisable by the system. By the prognosis. By the critics. He walked, he talked – albeit late and sometimes unintelligibly. He sat up until he found his teenage slouch, and he fed himself. A lot. And often. In fact, he's studying to be a chef. Dreaming of running his own restaurant. And I like to think I had a hand in that. But really, I know whose hand was truly holding him up.

Not to say that it wasn't hard and that we didn't have our challenges. I am bombarded with questions at least thirty times a day. His pre-frontal lobe completely inactive. And he blames and relies on me for his emotional state. And it's hard. It always has been. And there are times when I have been horrible to him. Vicious and abusive. Considering how vulnerable he is. And I can't even blame it all on the voices. That was something that lived within me. A spiteful anger and resentment at the life I had chosen in having him so young. And disgust in the fact that my identity was so wrapped up in him. And he was failing me with his disability. And his stupidity.

It's funny how one of the reasons we love our children is because of the absurd, narcissistic legitimacy it gives us. "I see so much of myself in her". When she's being exceptional, that is. Maybe that's why once I was over my post-natal depression and rid of my abusive relationship, I saw so much more of myself in Callum. My intelligent, vivacious, multidimensional, dynamic, well-integrated, thoughtful, witty, manipulative, arrogant, vain child. Maybe it was because my parenting efforts were so much more visible in him.

I have always wished to create a dynasty in my family that finally allows my ancestors to rest. One that cures the family of its generational trauma. But this comes with sacrifice and the desire to do better, love better and give what is needed. What you never got. So that the next generation can thrive rather than survive.

I have always prided myself on parenting in a manner that sought to simultaneously understand a child's world while explaining ours. Hoping that there could be forged a bridge of reasoning between the two. That our differences weren't so irreconcilable. I learnt through my own experiences how important it is for you, as the lead, to truly explore your child's inner universe, whilst encouraging them to explore the outer. And guide and support them in understanding it and their own. I longed to do this more with Joshua, but only patently achieved it with Callum.

If transparency is the key to personalised parenting, then humility is the tool. The ability to apologise for your own failures, your faults and your selfish nature is imperative in developing a relationship that is honest and open and progressive. No child is too young to understand pain. To see you as you are. If you let them. And no child is too young to understand themselves, if you can just hear them and teach them to listen. So I used all my learned knowledge to understand Callum's humanistic development and all I had personally learned to prepare him for the world. We spoke at length. Always. About all things him and us and them. I carefully facilitated the formation of his identity and cautiously reprimanded his egoistic state.

By the age of six he was critically self-reflective and fully comprehending of the human psyche. Able to spot an autistic child in the playground a mile away, or a person wordlessly crying out in need. Able to manage and reprimand bullies in a manner that recognised their hurt but taught fairness, equality and compassion. And able to both hate and forgive his father for his ultimate dismissal of him. His unexpected, completely expected, abandonment. By age nine having a greater grasp of the complexity and incompleteness that spurred on his father's behaviour, than his father.

He was my greatest achievement. A masterpiece, painted of my own sweat and toil, mixed into glorious watercolour with the intellect gleaned from my role in children's services. But just like every portion of my life thus far, just like all my childhood and adult friendships and just like my role as the adoring mother whose children "mean the world to me", something was missing. Something intrinsic in the meeting of minds. In the meshing of souls. This only truly accomplished when you are actually inhabiting yourself. And I knew it.

So despite knowing a part of me was lost somewhere, in a me that was lost also, in a time long ago, I worked hard to foster my children. To foster all children. And work was the place to do it. To prove myself. To disprove myself. Living and working under the guise that it was my compassion alone that spearheaded my commitment to children's emotional and psychological needs. And in many ways, it was.

I love children. I love them. I am filled with joy and unabated compassion whenever I am around them. I feel it spreading, like warmth across my chest. Like sinking into a warm bath. Soothing, consuming, comforting. Kindness and gentleness for them fills up my heart, and the authenticity of my smile can be easily felt by all those who witness it and returned by those it is intended for. I'm always the first to offer to play, or to spot when they're scared, or lonely, or upset. And I converse with them like they really mean something. I love their little faces and their silly ways. I love the way their minds work. The crazy things they think and say and the fact that it's not really that crazy when you think about it. I love how they are free. To think. To feel. To play. To love. To be. I validate them as unique, purposeful beings. I validate and adore them. And their love and adoration in return validate me.

People always say that animals and babies can tell. They know a bad egg by the look in their eyes, by the way they move, by their smell. By their very presence. They can take one look at a charlatan and cut through any façade. Sending out clear warning signals. Signified in the indignant bark of a dog or the strangled cry of an infant.

Toddlers run and hide from you and seek the security of their own parents, confining themselves to the parameters of their safe space. Unless, of course, their parent is the perpetrator. And there is no safe space. But that's developmental ideology. And the complexity of disordered attachments is a complicated theory. What needs to be understood, though, is that the security of a healthy and well-established attachment fosters learning about how to be resilient to the ever-changing, ever-challenging world. They learn how to predict others due to understanding, firstly, their parent's moods, secondly their own and then eventually all others they come into contact with. They have the confidence in themselves and their familiar safe space to return to when the world becomes a scary and harmful place. A space manned by a comforting being, who understands and prepares them to return again.

But for the toddler, it's not theoretical. It's visceral. It's in the blood. It's known without being known. And the innateness of their knowingness is defiantly executed in the face of every adult they come into contact with. For me, luckily, it offered reassurances that I was OK. That I was accepted. That I was one of the good guys.

Wasn't I?

Because how much power do you think you can gain with this sacred knowledge? How simply can a child be manipulated? Given they are, at the end of the day, just a child. Surely it's possible to fake it, to know what signals to send out? How to act? How to respond? How to present yourself? Physically and emotionally. So that you can be accepted. Validated. Authenticated. If you're into that kind of thing.

And it wasn't just at work. Not just with other people's kids that I did it. I shamefully used my own children to validate myself. I did the very thing I accused my parents of doing. But in a more sophisticated web of lies. I prided myself on being a good parent. Yes, because I really wanted to be. Yes, because I loved them. Yes, because I truly championed their happiness. But mainly because I needed the validation that being loved by a child gave. Because I needed to be needed. And there's no better people to be needed by than children. Because that makes it real, right?

I see now that there was so much missing in me. I had given up my dreams of superstardom for the lowly existence of social working. Of motherdom. Of martyrdom. And with it, my already shaky belief that I was anything of any worth. My loneliness and my unhappiness were invariably wrapped up in feelings of being trapped by my children and my life, and feeling unworthy of friends, comfort, support or love. I didn't try to make many other connections, and the ones I made only amplified my internalised feelings of worthlessness. I lessened my importance in the eyes of all those who did give me the time of day, because in my eyes, I already inhabited that space. It became that my children were my only friends. And I relied on them and resented them simultaneously. And I was dejected and miserable.

Tony Robbins says that when you're unhappy in your life, it's usually because the thing you're unhappy about doesn't match the blueprint of what you expected your life to be. However, that true suffering comes when you feel helpless and powerless to do anything about it. So you have three choices.

1) You can blame yourself and others. I did this a lot. I blamed my children. for trapping me in this lonely life and for becoming my only comfort. I blamed my mother for her emotionally void parenting and my father for his void in my life. I blamed my partner for his happiness, for his vivacious character and his abundance of friends. And I blamed the small number of friends I did have for the lack of real feeling I gained from our friendships. For not hailing me as the most important relationship in their lives and for not legitimising my existence through their commitment to me and our alliance. And I blamed myself. For not being good enough to have anyone around me who actually coveted my time. And for never really meaning anything to anyone. Something to someone. For wanting it, but never really knowing what *it* was.

2) If that's not working for you, you can always change your blueprint. As this is just our own projection of what we think we need to be happy. But there is what we think we need and what we actually, genuinely crave. What we long for. And what was that with me? Wanting friends, my children, other people's children to make me worthy? Wanting a partner that worshipped me alone? Wanting to be

liked, hailed, exulted? Wanting a good and powerful job? Wanting to have been famous. Wanting to have done more. Achieved more.

Wanting what?

Needing what?

Craving what?

Recognition.

Searching in all these different roles to be recognised as a person who means something.

To not be overlooked.

To be told I'm good enough.

Just as I am.

To feel good enough.

To know, instinctively, I am good enough.

And the minute that that is questioned through someone not texting me back, or not being invited out, or my friends talking amiably about a friend that I don't know, or feeling like my kids are my life, or being 'rejected' by my boyfriend because he needs space. I am immediately filled with fear.

Unabated fear.

And I start tumbling out of control. And I start scrambling for meaning and recognition and then feel guilty at my pride and arrogance. Feeling sickened by my desperation and pathetic-ness.

And then they've got me. In a low vibration of fear and shame. Where I feel like not even God would recognise me.

And He made me in his image.

He put His toil and sweat into the minutiae of my being. Intricately weaving every fibre of my body and lovingly constructing every minutia of my character.

And *that's* the place where the nightmares lived. In the depths of my fear. In the place where I never dared to look. Because it was too painful to think about the why. The real reason why I loved children so much. Where the real satisfaction was. So my head, my heart and my soul were filled with my worst nightmare. That my needs came from a dark, wicked, demonic place. That my drive, the catalyst for my commitment to, my love of my own and everyone else's children was twisted, immoral, heinous, inequitable and satanic at its core.

That I was wicked at my core.

3) Should the above leave you struggling to hold onto your reality, then you have the option to change it. It's scary though. Working as a social worker. A keeper of the peace. A pioneer of children's rights. Staring into the face of abusers, neglecters, assaulters and paedophiles day after day with a deep, dark secret of your own.

I used to lie awake at night. Praying to a God I never really believed was there. For answers. For peace. For atonement. I used to go back into the tattered catalogues of my forgotten childhood. Was I? Was there anyone? Did my dad? Was all that was said in venomous anger by his mistress true? Did my dad sexually assault me? Was my mum complicit in it? Was I assaulting my stepbrother? I can't remember doing that. But the problem was, I couldn't remember. Surely not. Surely, I would have had fewer problems breaking my hymen when I did finally do *the do*. Even if it only had lasted thirty seconds before my cousin burst into the room in the comical and horrendous style only she could achieve. Surely I would remember *something*.

What I can remember though is believing, vehemently, that there was something very, very wrong with me. I can remember believing, fervently, that I must have locked something, something really, really bad away. Deep, deep, deep in the depths of my unconscious. I had studied Freud. I understood how the unconscious worked. I knew the meaning of dreams. I knew what repression was and how it operated and how it bleeds out in abstract pictures while we sleep when it has no other way of communicating with us. How it protects us from our worst nightmares. Except my worst nightmares weren't abstract pieces of fine art to titillate my curiosity. They weren't titillating at all. They were concretely repulsive. But surely they meant something, right?

So how do you change this? How do you change something so abhorrent? How do you alter your unconscious state? If you believe it really is you? And who do you turn to? Especially when you are charged with protecting the very people you are unconsciously harming?

It was bad enough living with the fear that I would be found out for being the victim of domestic abuse. It was bad enough that they might start implementing drug testing. But this. This was something that could never be proved, something that could never be tested for and something else altogether. Something I just had to live with.

Every day.

And it was excruciating.

I was alone again. But in my heart, rightly so. And I was tortured and driven insane by what I felt was my own mind. I couldn't bear myself, and I feared sleep and a world I where I was powerless, where I couldn't control or push down or repress. Because you can't repress the repression. You can't repress the oppression. Because even though Freud is the epitome of sophisticated psychotherapy, much of what he wrote isn't even empirically based and just the ramblings of a mad man who psychoanalysed himself. And there is an entire age, an entire lifetime when it was accepted that a dream was something that came to you. Not out of you.

After my salvation one of the first things I did was to check. To think and contemplate. To muse and percolate. To stare into my soul. Directly into my soul and directly at the fear. To ask the question I had always been too afraid to hear the answer to. Am I damned? And what I found was sweet, divine and delirious redemption. Nothing of the abhorrence I was plagued with in my past. Nothing of the wicked monstrousness, the iniquity, the evil, the sin I believed I was. Because that's what it feels like now. A past life. There are no more dreams and nothing even recognisable of that part of me.

Because it wasn't me. It was something else. Something that fled the minute Jesus' name was whispered into my ear.

And it is not me.

It is not me.

It is not me.

And I am free.

25 June 2020

A whole week of bliss. A whole week of calm, of peace, of happiness. Spent searching for the rot and finding nothing but boundless space to fall, backwards, open arms into. Silence in my head and joy on my lips. Courtney keeps asking if it's definitely gone, fear and anxiety in his eyes. It's not even irritating. I love him. I'm filled with the spirit. I am love. I am forgiveness. I am compassion. I just want to embrace the world. I want to sing. To run. To praise with my hands open to the heavens.

The feeling of holding my son for the first time brings tears to my eyes. I am unstoppable. Fearless. Excited and grateful for all the opportunities that lay ahead of me, easily formed and clearly seen in my mind's eye. I'm in bliss. No more whisperings. No more rot. No more twisting, turning hand in my stomach. The exhaustion of having to battle to find myself every moment of every day done. The battle is won. The existence of God is real, and I am blessed to truly know Him. We speak regularly, and I cherish Him. I feel Him all around me. I personally know my God and have nothing but unwavering faith in the fact. The fact that He loves me. I am bursting at the seams and have never felt so powerful and so humbled.

I tell all that will listen. Hear my story. Witness my salvation. Live my redemption. Trouble is, the more I force it, the more *the story loses its power. And that's what it starts to become. A story. An anecdote. Not just out of my mouth, but in my mind also. Everyone keeps telling me I'm special. I'm chosen. I'll save many. And lead them to God. This is my ministry. And vanity creeps in. How lucky is Courtney? To be sat next to me! I am a Saviour. I am a Prophet. I will cure and lead the nations! And vanity creeps in. And my ego slowly starts to outweigh the power of Jesus. The mercy of God. And the joy of the Holy Spirit.*

So where do I eventually find myself? Untouchable. And high on ketamine in my room. Again, a cocktail of drugs coursing through my mind and my body. But it's fine. In fact, it's beautiful. God is still loud in my head, and my connection to Him, Courtney and the Universe is unbreakable. Isn't it? Just another bump. It can't hurt me. Nothing can. Right?

Until I fall. I tumble. I plummet. Out of myself. And into an abyss. I'm not there anymore. My faculties, my body, my mind. They're not my own. They have been vacated. So I watch on in frozen horror as multiple shadows crawl across my bedroom wall, converging into one horrendous monstrosity. And shoot directly into my gut. I'm hit. I feel it immediately. The pain. The rot. My body is full of them. And I'm in agony. I frantically start searching for God, but I am disabled. Watching helplessly on as I'm filled with fear. And doubt. And fear. "God save me", I cry out silently.

I can feel the battle taking place inside me. All around me. Only, I'm not on the field. I missed the call. I wasn't in. No one's at home. And the enemy knew it. Knew just when to strike. What did Pastor Peters say? "Then he goes, and takes seven other spirits more evil than himself and they enter and dwell there." But only if you've left it empty. If it isn't filled with Him.

I was warned. Warned to fill my soul, my mouth, my life with God. Warned that if I left myself open, this thing. This monstrous thing would come to reclaim its home. Its mouth. Its mind.

And now, here I am, pregnant with pomposity, ego and vanity. So juiced up with my own pride that I am completely incapacitated. And now my soul is under fire. My life is in the balance. Because I know going back to that is death. First I will die, and then I will kill myself. And then. Without my doing. Without my help. Without my input. The battle is done. He has conquered. Again. He has fought and died for me. Again. And the battle is won.

Isn't it?

The battle always has been won, hasn't it?

Then why do I feel this? Why has the pain come back? Creeping up on me like a sinister fiend, down a dark alleyway on a dark night. Why am I searching and finding nothing but terror? I am terrorised. I am forsaken. I'm desperate. I'm wretched. "Please, God. Please, God. Please, God", I scream through muted lips. And a deafening mind. Head up, hands out. Hot, thick tears falling like burning suffering down my face.

I have been forsaken.

And it's exactly what I deserve.

What if, Three

WHAT IF, 3) **IT DIDN'T TAKE AN EXORCISM TO WAKE YOU UP? IF BEAUTY, FAME, FORTUNE AND POWER WEREN'T THE ONLY THINGS THAT MATTERED? WHAT IF YOU REALISED YOUR EGO AND VANITY WERE JUST THE REMNANTS OF A BEAUTIFUL GIFT OFFERED TO YOU TO SERVE YOURSELF AND OTHERS. AND IT BECAME CLEAR WHY, AND BY WHOM, ITS PURPOSE HAD BEEN CORRUPTED?**

WHAT IF YOU HAULED BACK THE VEIL TO REVEAL THAT GOOD AND EVIL ACTUALLY EXISTED?
WHAT IF YOU WOKE UP AND REALISED WHO'S SIDE YOUR IGNORANCE HAD CHOSEN FOR YOU?

WOULD YOU CHOOSE AGAIN?

I've always been told I was pretty. From a very young age. Research tells us that children who are more aesthetically pleasing suffer less long-lasting affects from adverse childhood experiences. Because they are receiving something like positive regard from somewhere. Being validated in some way. Some of the time.

With no balance, though, nothing real or meaningful or palpable to hold onto, this can be just as damaging. Your beauty becomes a symbol of your worth, and invariably you know of nowhere else to get the recognition.

And it's hard. When you are actually aesthetically pleasing. To let it go. To find something deeper or more eloquent to give you worth. It's like a quick fix. A needle directly into the vein. To the root of the problem. Yes! I mean something! I. Am. Beautiful.

And it's even harder when you live in a society that is obsessed, completely preoccupied, completely fixated on beauty. When we are told that this is what gives our life meaning, this is what will take us to the next level. Wherever that is. Because beauty's certainly not a prerequisite to entering the gates of heaven, not the kind that you find on the outside anyway.

Not that anyone is trying to get there anymore. Stay young and beautiful. Stay here on earth. Soaking up the adoration of your fellow beauty enthusiast, and all the common folk. There's nothing better than this. This *is* heaven on earth.

All my life as a young woman I have wrestled with my own beauty. With coveting and dismissing it. I have always wanted to be accepted for who I am. For more than just how I look. For my intellect. And my dry wit. And my kind heart. And my compassion for others. And my love of people. And my helpful nature. And all my redeeming qualities.

And my hot body.

And my beautiful face.

I have always endeavoured to be a girl's girl. A woman's woman. I am a feminist, and of course my alliances are with my fellow female. I would never covet the attention of another woman's man. Or sit up just that little bit straighter whenever they were around. Or inwardly smile to myself in response to their sly looks and their covert compliments. Relishing the glares of accusation and envy. Why can't you be more like her? More fun, more chilled, more easy-going, more down, more funny, more demure, more couture.

And of course, I am not so pompous to believe that I could have your boyfriend if I wanted him. That I could have any man I wanted.

Because the truth is, I am a woman's woman. I would never actively steal anyone's man. I would never actively lead anyone on, and I abhor cheaters. I hate to see others in pain, and I could never be the cause of another woman's downfall. My enduring love for Courtney being the only deplorable exception. I have, however, supposed some really bad things. Had some really low thoughts on the tip of my tongue on multiple occasions. When my eyes are as resolutely set forward as my allegiances to the female race.

I'm not proud of it. It's not who I ever wanted to be. It's my nemesis. My sin. It was just so easy, so simple, so *right there*. Easily grabbed and held onto, like a buoy in the sea of loneliness and confusion that was my childhood. Where I was never told I was good enough, just as I am. And it replenished me in a way that nothing else did. And it stuck. Like flies to shit.

Vanity is such a tricky one. On the one hand the more I read about Jesus, the more I realise he was confident, often to the point of arrogance. In his position, his power and his authority. But never vain. Whereas I was taught that any self-confidence was sinful. I was taught to make myself as small as possible so that my gifts would never overshadow or undermine someone still searching for theirs.

Because, ultimately, they would only be searching for something that they already have. Because God is never stingy in the gifts He gives us. He has provided each and every one of us with something that we can use to channel our sorrow and restabilise ourselves. To purge ourselves of pain and flush out any rot. Before it grows so great it overcomes you. And you have to be exorcised by your boyfriend on the couch on a Wednesday night.

For me it was singing. I was given the most blessed gift. The most beautiful talent. The most profound voice. I was smashing Whitney out of the park by the age of nine. Leaving audiences flabbergasted and awestruck on the small number of occasions I actually found the confidence to open my mouth. I was six the first time I was told I could sing, and she meant *really* sing. My friend's mum, a singer herself, bowled over and gushing about the maturity in my voice.

But it was a sin in my house to promote any of this. Even now I am still uncomfortable discussing my talents in any positive way. Opting for the more familiar, 'oh, it's not that big of a deal really' type stance. And as a result, any time I am called on to sing, I suffer immobilising stage fright. I was berated for singing in the house by my mother, politely reminded that nobody else wanted to hear that. That I should be considerate of other people's feelings. I sometimes wonder if it was hers she was referring to. And I was wheeled out once in a while for my father's friends. Or forced through gritted teeth and daggered shoulder digs to get up and karaoke when I was too overcome with fear. But always asked why I wouldn't just shut the fuck up singing all the time. At all other times.

When I was alone, I would sing though. I don't think anyone has heard the true extent of my voice other than me. And God of course. Sometimes I would sing til I cried. Waves of emotion washing over me and out of me until I felt pacified. And I, like David in the desert, had intrinsically known from a young age the power of healing someone's voice could have, my voice could have, if I let it. But it was never enough. I wanted the acclamation. I wanted the praise. I wanted the awe and the envy and the power myself. I wanted to hear from others' lips that I was talented and amazing and incredible.

So eventually, the crushing feeling that I wasn't acknowledged, let alone celebrated by either of my parents; the discomfort of singing to other people's tunes; and the inherent need for recognition merged together, to turn something that was given for good, the good of me and the good of others. For healing. A remedy. A melody. And twisted it into an ugly something used for my own sanctification. My trump card. Another way to feel and be better than all the others. Even if it was permanently glued to my chest.

This never the more obvious than the eight-year period of my life when I couldn't sing. After I gave it up. Desperately focussing on completing my university degree. After getting kicked out and setting a president of being *the only* student let back in. After submitting to real life. And after abandoning my dreams and the belief that there was anything more exciting out there for me.

Nothing but strangled air exhaled whenever I tried to form a note. Formed to remind me of my loss. And with it the feeling that a part of my soul had died. So I stopped appreciating music. Stopped listening to it altogether. Jealous and green of other people's talents, other people's gifts. And my inability to match up to the bar I had set for myself. Like a spoilt toddler sulking about the toy they never even wanted, now entertaining the contented infant sat next to them. And it exposed that this talent wasn't so much about my soul as my ego.

I had never grown to healthily embrace the thing put here for me to channel my pain. Or inspire others. And praise His name. And as a result, there formed a void that I couldn't quite grasp. That I didn't quite understand. And in that void grew conceited arrogance. Pride. Vanity. Ego. Superego. And eventually, an alter ego.

Frankly, with men and their women, it made me feel better to know I was wanted. Desired. That I could make a man fall in love with me in an instant. That I was better than others. And with my voice, that I had a gift that would put others to shame. Even if I could barely share it with the world. In my head. I was the queen of the night. Just like honey. What you want? Baby, I got it.

And even if I could never walk the boards of a real stage, my mind and my life were an amphitheatre. Built just for me. Solo act. Headlining. I pranced around, performing for the crowd, and collected bouquets. And pinned a rosette on my breast for each person I secretly bested. With my God-given gifts.

I can remember a friend asking how I exuded so much confidence. *Exuded* being the operative word. And my confusion when she said that acting as though someone was always watching you was not her kind of thing. Whose kind of thing wasn't it? It was unbelievable, novel even, to me that this was not everyone's remedy to feeling worthless. That other people weren't proactively tangled in their own web of lies and deception. Deceiving themselves and others about their own importance in the world.

But I guess that's just conditions of worth for you. Or conditions of worthlessness. Carl Rogers asks us all to consider where our locus of evaluation lives. Internally or externally? Within or without? Based on who you think *you* should be? Or who you think you *should* be?

Carl proposes we have all fashioned our worlds and ourselves through the internalisation of the world around us, in a manner that reflects the expectations of, essentially, our parents, amongst others. And how we construct our world is based entirely upon the way we see it. And the way we see it is the way it was presented to us. From the beginning. What is good. What is bad. How we should measure ourselves based upon a fictitious barometer passed down from generation to generation. Therefore, our values are introjected, or the tendency to "unconsciously adopt the ideas or attitudes of others".

And my family values taught that there was only one way to live. A narrow path of their very own. To be walked like a muzzled mule, broken in and blinkered. And *that* was my mother's way. As well as my father's way. As well as by the rules of society. Whilst also not by society's rules, because they are racist. But never, ever by my own way.

So how do you ever find your own voice, excuse the pun, in the midst of that? How do you ever know what you represent? Or how to represent it? How do your own conditions of worth get fulfilled? How are your conditions of unworthiness overcome? How do you make yourself feel better?

Well, what you do is, you make rules in your own head. About what is good and what is bad. About what is better and what is worse. And then you apply them to everyone. And measure yourself upon them. You place everyone at the starting blocks of a race they never signed up for and then you pit yourself against them. Silently. Stealthily. Seethingly. And occasionally, victoriously.

Freud tells us that ego comes before the superego but after the id. It is the development of the self. The recognition that you are a unique and purposeful being. That beyond being fed and watered, you have a mind and a view and a voice. Freud, however, also believes we are all destined to self-satisfaction, self-sanctification, and stimulated by primitive desire and greed and aggressive instinct. The ego, playing the role of a perfunctory public relations officer between the mighty dynasty that are our id and our superego, or the societal limitations to our innate depravity. But I believe the ego is the self in its most beautiful, innate form; however, when damaged or fractured in its early construction, it easily becomes an all-consuming, judgemental, arrogant personality. A way of navigating within a world in which, ultimately, you do not feel good enough.

You see ego everywhere. From the Hollywood superstar, to the playboy stockbroker, to the benevolent philanthropist. You see ego in the church. In the pomposity of religion. And all the men who have made war from it. In the anointed hands of every man ordained by God. Placing those anointed hands over the sick and weary. It's not a verb. A thing that you do. That you have. "That must be my ego talking", they all say. But it's not. It's not 'The Ego'. It just the thin-layered façade of all these people. All these souls. In their pathetic attempts to mask their own insignificance and their own misgivings.

And it was nowhere more blatant than in me, after my salvation. I went from saved to Saviour. I was overripe for it. Like pungent-smelling fruit turned to wine. To feed that undeserving wedding party. I had finally arrived. Finally, it's happened to me! This was it. This was my calling all along. This is why I was chosen. This is what I am here for. And aren't you all so lucky. You, Courtney. Sat next to a master. A prophet, some might say. And with that, all my humble thanks, my gracious appreciation was blown out of the water to make way for my massive head.

Because even though I had gained life through Jesus. I had lost so much of myself, and all I had previously relied upon. All that I felt important to get there. My barometer was broken and my judgement was off. So I had no other way of knowing that I was any longer powerful. Any longer meaningful, because vanity, pride, ego, these are all ways of us reassuring ourselves that we have some power in our own lives. All the more understandable in those who have felt sustained powerlessness.

The ego especially tells you that you need power. The world and our society tell you that you need power. And in my salvation I had augmented mine. Recognising all along that toying with men and toying with fame wasn't right. And recognising that invariably all judgement just comes from a feeling of not measuring up, and measuring up others so you can pull them down to beneath you. Thus, through our own conditioned and conditional world, we decide that we're better than 'them'. And ultimately, if you're actually a half-decent person, feel pretty shitty about it.

And as I now know. With unrivalled certainty and blinding clarity. This is a dangerous vibration. This is the binary where susceptibility turns into compulsion. And being compelled by another, something set apart from your alter ego, something more angry and scornful and jealous and spiteful than you could ever be, even at your worst. Something that takes all these ugly, obnoxious characteristics and amplifies them to a point whereby you are unrecognisable. Distorted and grotesque. Being compelled by this is death. Because first you die and then you kill yourself.

Vanity is a sin. Not because of the harm it does to us on the outside, but because of the harm it does to us on the inside. From the inside out. And deeper into the inside still. Vanity makes you hateful and scornful of yourself and others and masks itself as "the quality of being important". It's not a quality. It qualifies you for iniquity.

Vanity is defined in the dictionary as 'unaccountable' and 'disapproving'. No wonder, then, we are unaccountable in our disapproval of others. In the Bible vanity is described as a deadly sin.

Not because it's bad. Or naughty. Or looks ugly and unpleasant and unbecoming. But because it creates major divides for us from God. It distracts us from who really is doing bits for us. It convinces us that we are the almighty. The all-powerful. The grand designer of our own destiny. We are untouchable and formidable in our authority and glory.

But if you can have the humility, to truly see yourself and one another. As we are. If you have the humility to accept what was written. For each of us. That God loves you. Made you worthy. Shares all with you.

Is love.

That we are made from that love and in His image and with the exact tools we need. That there is no difference, no divide, no hierarchy between us. We are each inhabiting this place in the exact manner needed, with the exact gifts, tools and weapons for the job.

And the job is love, not destruction.

The job is peace, not anarchy and rebellion. Against each other. Against ourselves. Or against God. That there is nothing to be jealous of and there is nothing to be vain for. That our ego is nothing but the whisperings of a person constructed through the oppression and opposition of living in *this* family. *This* society. *This* world.

But that this is not God's world.

That He wants to save us.

To keep us.

To bring us together and to love us.

And he wants us to love each other and ourselves.

Because it's exactly what we deserve.

30 June 2020

It's back. It took three days to admit it to myself, even though I knew it the very instant it happened. I am undone. I deserve it. I am a lowly wretch who took for granted the miracle gifted to me by the Lord. I feverishly search the Bible. For inspiration. For the feeling I've lost. In my mind. In my doubt, my fear and my pain. What did I expect? That I was truly loved? Truly forgiven? Actually saved?

I can't even recall the memory of my experience. My redemption. The feeling of grace. And the events that took place just over a week ago seem like a movie. Black-and-white reels, watched and long forgotten in the memories of my youth. I am nothing. I am damned. Damned to live this life. With these things. Inside my head and my heart and my gut. Where did you go, God? Please come back. Come back and save me. I need you. I am desperate, devasted and completely demoralised. Completely demonised. I beseech you every waking moment to show yourself to me.

All hope is lost and the promise of the life I knew before is gone. The light is hidden from me, and a cloud of depression once again hangs over me. Like the weighted blanket used to root me back to the earth. The difference now, though, is palpable, unmistakable. And the voices are deafening in my ear. I'm pregnant, pungent, permeating with fear. I can feel it *coursing through my blood like a disease. One I know will surely kill me. And I deserve it. Useless, worthless human being. Courtney is beside himself. He is finally out of ideas, and we stare at each other with knowing fear. Petrified at what is to become of us. I'm too ashamed to even ask for help. To speak aloud my humiliated state, my mistake. My ungrateful error.*

So we sit. Trying to figure out what the pastor meant when he said I was forever saved. And God told him I never needed to worry again. Surely God wouldn't forsake me like this. Would He?

The nightmares return, and I finally wake on the fourth day ready to accept my fate and this reality. Only, in the acceptance of it, I find a strange kind of peace. Like finally receiving the bad news you already knew was coming. Accepting the cancer with relief. Something almost bordering relish.

So if it's back, then it's not me. It's not my voice that cries out. It's not my thoughts that plague me. It's the deceiver. The father of all lies. The tormentor. Returned in a furious rage and feigned glory to retake his stake on my soul. How clever you are. Almost convincing me again that I am unloved, unworthy and unwanted. How clever you are. But how you have underestimated me. Underestimated God. Underestimated the power of Jesus and the truth that I can only be forever saved.

The realisation of the power and the wisdom of God, and how significantly this has been misjudged by the enemy is almost comical. How clever He is! Using His enemies to do His work. Allowing, even encouraging, my fear and despair. Knowing, ultimately, that it would lead me back to Him.

My faith is more than renewed. It is solidified as I cling to my God. Relishing the strength, power and authority He brings. Welcoming the journey and marvelling at the Grand Designer and his grand design for me. Who knew all roads led to Him? And that faith was the only guide? Unwavering, immeasurable faith. Without reassurance. Without understanding. Without any true awareness of the destination. Just an unbreakable belief, confidence and conviction in the covenant God wrote before you were born. That you are saved. You are loved. You are redeemed. You are His.

What if, Four

WHAT IF, 4) **IT DIDN'T TAKE AN EXORCISM TO WAKE YOU UP? IF EVERYONE ELSE WASN'T THE ENEMY AND YOU COULD, ACTUALLY, FIND SALVATION THROUGH FORGIVENESS? WHAT IF YOU DIDN'T SCOFF AT THE IDEA OF BEING SAVED AND SALVATION WAS THE ONLY SALVATION? AND IT WAS ONLY GAINED THROUGH LOVING THOSE YOU LOVE TO HATE? WHAT IF YOU REALISED THAT YOUR HATRED AND SCORN AND DISMISSAL OF YOUR FELLOW MAN WAS SOMETHING WOVEN INTO THE FABRIC OF OUR SOCIETY FOR A DEDICATED PURPOSE?**

WHAT IF YOU YANKED BACK THE VEIL TO REVEAL THAT GOOD AND EVIL ACTUALLY EXISTED? WHAT IF YOU WOKE UP AND REALISED WHO'S SIDE YOUR IGNORANCE HAD CHOSEN FOR YOU?

WOULD YOU CHOOSE AGAIN?

On my sixth birthday my dad left. I don't remember much, but I do remember coming home to find the house covered in photographs. How strange and wonderful I must have thought, on first impression. What a weird way to celebrate my birthday, throwing our family photos everywhere. But, hey, OK, you're the parents. I guess you know what you're doing. I can still vaguely remember the visceral shock moving from my fingers up my arm and into my heart as they pinched the first picture of my family, my dad ripped out. And the second and the third. Happy birthday, Fran. Welcome home. And welcome to the world.

My parents had never been happy. I don't think. I don't have any memories of them together, though, so I just have to take their slander for it. I do remember the pan incident though. Waking up to screaming and shouting downstairs, my mum not looking like my mum and my brother on the stairs, telling me not to go down there and that everything would be alright. He couldn't have been more than five or six himself. But he was always wiser than me. I could just about manage the stairs confidently. My little four-year-old legs still shaky at times. Plates were being smashed, and the big black frying pan. The one made of iron. Something I can't remember happened with that.

Other than this lovely snippet, they have, in my memory, always been apart. And dedicatedly at war. They didn't speak once in nearly ten years. After they split up. Didn't utter a word to one another. So strong was their dislike for one another. Until they banded together to convince me into my abortion. What a beautiful ceremony to bring my parents back into communion. Glad to have been the vessel in their happy reunion.

My mum had entered into a new, and no doubt, healthier relationship, within months of their separation, and my dad had started his whilst still sleeping in the cold and empty marital bed. According to the scriptures.

And so, aged seven begun in our house the era of Thomas Robertson. A strange and desperate man, some fourteen years younger than my mum, but already balding and cynical. It's funny because my mum often accused my father of physical abuse, but the truth is we all know it was Tom who perpetrated that type of control over the household. But like most battered women, I guess she liked the affirmation the good bit of the domestic abuse cycle gave her.

I could never put my finger on it, as I never saw anything, but the house was pungent with atmosphere. Something that I couldn't quite grasp. Something that was just beyond the reaches of my infantile mind. But something that made those standalone crazy times seem quite unremarkable, expected almost.

The first taste of crazy followed another clandestine argument and stealthy separation. He, unable to accept his fate, made the decision to jump back garden fences to remove and then reconstruct the dated, individual sliding windowpanes in my kitchen. Each no bigger than an adult's forearm, but when all detached large enough to squeeze an average-sized man through. Clearly.

I again woke to screaming and shouting. No pan this time. Instead, my mum frantically pleading with a desperately crazed Thomas Robertson to give back the keys and let us out of the house. It was like slow motion. My eight-year-old brain not quite comprehending the seriousness of the situation but instinctively knowing it was bad. Really bad. My brother, the sensible and wise child he was, immediately went to search for the house phone. And finding nothing but the markings of where it used to be, returned looking slightly more stricken.

So we all retreated into the hallway, regrouped. Decided on a game plan, a plan of action, a strategy of attack. Me and mum would grab him as soon as we saw an opening and, using all our might, wrestle him to the ground. Matt would spring into action, fingering his pockets for the house keys. And run, like our lives depended on it (because they did) to the front door. We would hold him off as long as possible to give Matt the time he needed to unlock the front door and run as far from the house as he could. Ready? And, break!

I can remember clinging onto his arm for dear life. The back of my head bouncing off the corner of our concrete fireplace. Determined not to let go. Matt said that the woman using the phone box was rightly concerned to see a pyjama-clad nine-year-old, eyes wide open with fear and struggling for breath from his lactic-filled lungs. When the police finally came, we were sent to bed. And it was never spoken of again. Or the fact that he was back around the dinner table within a matter of weeks.

Not that my mum took it lying down. I mean, he did camp outside the front door. Blocking our only route in and out of the house. In a one-man tent. Declaring words of love and regret nonstop through the letterbox. For two days. And when he finally did return home, he did tie up the phone line by refusing to end the call on his side. So that instead of the familiar dial tone, his hopeful and expectant 'Barbaras?' became the familiar sound whenever we lifted the receiver. Surely that kind of commitment deserved a second chance, right? And I'm pretty sure there was a holiday in it somewhere for my mum. A romantic destination where she could lose her cares, her worries. Herself. And forget all about it. We, of course, remained at home. Staring at the spot where it happened.

There was also that time they barricaded themselves in respective bedrooms. We didn't have locks on our bedroom doors. Because we were that open and inviting kind of a family unit, I guess. Them both utilising the other's toilet breaks to steal or resteal items procured from occupied enemy land. We watched on for a while before we called the police. And watched on again while they slowly negotiated the hostage situation. "Barbara, Thomas has agreed to return your keys if you will agree to give him back his passport". It was a delicate operation. I hope the coppers had received their hostage negotiation training.

But aside from the big crazies, there was just always a general feeling of unrest. Maybe because the relationship was strained and we all could feel it. Maybe because their arguments were quiet and vicious. Imperceptible almost. Or maybe because we weren't allowed to talk about the things that had happened to us. It was forbidden. Taboo. So we ate our veg and remembered our manners and really appreciated the opportunity for fresh air and frolics on our family nature walks. Thomas leading us on.

It was a strange and unsettling relationship to watch. A strange blueprint for intimate relationships. For personal strength. Or self-worth or respect. But I didn't know any better and had no other decent male role model to refer to, to endorse the vague notion that something wasn't right.

My dad was sporadic. At best. But constant in his denigration of my mum and my home life. On the weekends he bothered to turn up, he would spend much of his time coaching us. Reminding us of whose children we were. What colour we were. Who loved us most. Whose fault it was. What the judge had said and how the system was racist and against him. Sending us home with questions beyond the comprehension of our childlike minds. Recited to us over and over like a doctrine, a creed. His creed. So that we could 'get the truth'. Because we deserved it. And our mum was keeping it from us.

He spoke a lot about having lost the battle this time, but that he would eventually win the war. I didn't know I was in a war. But I was. We both were. Me and my big bro. We were pawns. Cannon fodder. Sent out and discarded in my parents' desperation to keep hold of their respective empires. My dad the brutish commander-in-chief, charging head-first into battle, and my mother the refined vizier, cunningly sneaking into your tent while you fought on. And poisoning your wine. And the wine of all your men.

He once refused to see us for six months because our grandmother's birthday card arrived late. A whole day late. I was perhaps six. I didn't know how a stamp worked. I can remember Friday nights searching the street, way past sundown. My little heart doing tiny leaps of hope whenever a headlight flashed. And feeling crushed whenever they drove on past my house or turned away from it. 'Saving All My Love' became my anthem, and I would sing it, unabandoned, every time he didn't turn up. Tears streaming down my bloated baby face.

Even though he forsook us. He saved nothing of himself for us. Except marching orders and control. My brother stood up to him once. After he turned up nearly three hours late. He refused to go with him. So my dad refused to take me and told me to blame it on my brother. He didn't see us for a long time after that. So my brother wrote to him, offering to pay for the cinema. In the hope he would turn up. For the free entertainment at least. I think he bestowed the honour on him.

Beyond the half-hearted excuses of work or car breakdowns, her refusal to enter into conversation about their divorce and consistent reminders that she was doing the best she could, my mum was stoical through it all. To the point of abuse. Never, ever speaking about anything. Ever. Opting for the higher road, where you feel righteous. And your children have no idea what the fuck's going on. Until she couldn't take it anymore and put us in a cab. In our pyjamas. Clothes in big black bin bags, and sent us away. Without the money for the fare, without the name or number plate of the driver, and without the foggiest idea whether anyone would be there to receive us on the other end. My brother advised me against taking sweets from strangers when we stopped to fill up for gas. And I ended up with pneumonia instead.

We were back at home within a week. It was the first time I saw my dad cry. A momentary glimpse behind the curtain as he walked past the front room window. Returning from the courthouse. He was angry by the time he was packing our things back up to leave. I think he cried for us, but it could have been for the loss of another battle. I hope it was for us, as we had clearly set up in opposing camps, my brother secretly playing for the other team. He was an informant. A mole. And my mum took all his lost cries for his home life and weaponised it against my dad. And I was a snitch in my own right, informing my dad of their secret phone calls while he was out of the house, and we were left unsupervised. My dad never forgave him after that. And I think my brother never forgave me.

And all this. Before the age of ten. So it was around this age that I decided that hope was for chumps. That it was better to keep your hopes, your dreams, your optimism to a minimum. That way, *when*, not *if*, you were let down, you would be much less disappointed. It would hurt so much less. You would recover so much more quickly. And crack on with real life.

But I guess they're the kind of decisions you make when nobody talks to you. Explains anything. Holds you. Physically or emotionally. Reminds you that all that you are experiencing isn't your doing, doesn't represent you as a person. Or represent that person's love for you. Or your entire worth as a human being.

But I guess you can only really do that if you are emotionally held yourself, and my mother was not. We had all we needed. Nicely ironed school clothes, healthy food, modified hydrogenated fat oil cut out of our diet, spoonfuls of cod liver, bedtime routines. Clean teethies, stories at bed, everything a growing child could need. Other than the knowledge that they are safe. And loved, no matter what.

I don't think my mother said she loved me consistently until I was at least twenty-eight, and that was following a dedicated and well-constructed campaign that lasted nearly six years. Including a year of me saying it to no reply, nearly two years of my saying it to a clipped and perfunctory thanks, and then a situation that got so socially awkward for my mother that her middle-class etiquette forced her to say it back. Another two years passing before that became anything near comfortable. And aged thirty-seven, it's still alien to our relationship.

I get it though. I understand her. She is from an age where psychological needs were for pussies; they just simply didn't exist, and children needing to have theirs met was something sublime. Like the start of a bad joke. The parent, the child and the elephant in the room walk into the doctor's office. In fact, her psychological needs are so far lost to her that she wouldn't even recognise she has any. Or what the hell I'm talking about.

Not that I am trying to deconstruct my mother. I don't know her well enough; we've never had that type of relationship. And I hear she's a really good friend and a nice person, but I can only imagine the difficulty of being the firstborn to an only child, spoilt, subsequent alcoholic Yorkshire lass/poverty-stricken, one of fourteen, two up two down, emotionally robotic Polish refugee of war. I can imagine how it felt to never, ever be told you did good enough by your father. That if you weren't first it meant nothing. To never be told that you were loved. To never have those words or those actions expressed to you in any way.

I can imagine how crushing it is to never be protected from your father's brutal admonitions because your mother was too busy drinking her own feelings away. Sulking at the fact that she was miserable with the hasty choices she had made. Married to, and seven children with, an emotionally repressed man because he bowed and clicked his heels the first time he asked you to dance. I can imagine how the restrictions and conditions placed around love in my mother's childhood home would cause emotional instability. All fostered within an era where you didn't acknowledge these things, let alone speak about them. And with it the inability to accept yourself or love others.

Thank God we had the ability to express ourselves by the time I was equally fucked up. Thank God I had weed and the opportunity to think outside of myself. And a friend who chewed the fat with me for seven years, and another for the next eight. Or I would have kept the cycle going. Because I don't even blame my grandparents; they've got their own story, their own baggage, their own pain. And so have their parents and so on and so forth. Abuse and neglect passing down to us like intangible genetic disorders.

Except it's not so intangible when you're living with the passive aggression and the scornful comments and the unfettered hatred that you have no idea from where it came. I can honestly say that no one is more horrible to me than my mum. No one is more abusive to me than the woman that birthed me. I tried to tell her recently. She scoffed at it. Apparently I've always got some issue. She was more telling in what she said than she realised though.

I started it. Apparently. This bitter feud. This cyclical vacuum of distance. When I was twelve and I chose my dad over her. And in every person that I have chosen over her since then. She is rejected.

Ultimately rejected. By the one person she thought she could rely on to love her, since her parents had made such a hash of it. And she doesn't even know. What she does know, however, is that I am the culprit; I am the instigator, the wrongdoer. I deserve her treatment of me, not that she knows what on earth I'm talking about. And I should be apologising for and acknowledging my decisions. As a twelve-year-old. Trapped in a bitter war.

Yes, of course she knows how to love. Of course love is the only way; Jesus says so. And she reads the Bible, and goes to church religiously, and helps out on the committee, and sets the 3:00 p.m. alarm for the hour of mercy. But she has no mercy for me. She knows how to love, she says. Just not me. Because, ultimately, I am a reminder of her own childhood trauma, and she can't bear to look at it.

And I know that she did love me once. I know that she made the 5:00 a.m. journey, every morning, to give me sustenance. Her milk. Her life. When I was still small and vulnerable, hospitalised and recovering from meningitis. And I know she got the bus each day, despite my dad's car sitting unused while he snoozed away at home. And I know that she probably suffered post-natal depression of her own, weary and forlorn from the exhaustion of bringing a child into the world all alone, even though you had a husband. And a failing marriage, the only support offered by strangers after being found one day, face down and crying at her desk. And I know that despite my father stealing her maternity checks and forging her signature, and despite his gambling addiction and his adultery, she stoically persevered. And I love and honour her for that. Even if we can't find it anymore. Even though it has been lost to us.

And it wasn't all bad at home. We had my cousins and Sundays at my grandma's house, her more settled and easy-going, and drunker in her old age. My grandfather still making alterations to the house, building extensions and sinks in every room at the ripe old age of seventy. Making up plays and feeding one another gruel and playing church and picking on and loving each other. We had each other. And it was a rock of normality in my life. In all of our lives, I think. Since all my cousins are made of the same stock. There were family holidays to Wales and trekking adventures with all of us kids, like a troupe, out to find mischief and mayhem. And I adored those days of my childhood.

Until they were over all too quickly. The life I knew shattered into inexistence in the summer of my first year of secondary school. My parents, of course, were not talking, so my brother was charged with negotiating visitation; having received no hostage negotiation training – other than witnessing the experts returning random possessions during the great stakeout of 1992 – and telling him he can't just call whenever he feels like it and swoop in and have you. And that he is not playing fair. And that we would not, under any circumstances, be available this weekend. And that she was sick of moving her arrangements around to suit him.

He clearly wasn't too adept at it because my dad turned up anyway, pompous and self-righteous in his court-directed rights to see his children. My mum ineffectively dragging us back by our arms and clothes upon his arrival. Placing her hands in front of us and all over us in a desperate struggle to maintain some control and self-respect. So Thomas Robertson locked us in the house. And told my dad in his polite, *Sunday Guardian*–reading, superior manner that we would not be coming out; and subsequently got punched in the face and thrown into a bush. My brother, the wise one, climbed out of the window. And I, wide-eyed with wonder, followed. The police had been called by then and being of sound mind and body asked us where we wanted to go. It had been a time since my dad had been around, so we both chose him. Aged twelve.

We returned to my mum missing, my house empty of all contents and a 'for sale' sign posted outside of the front gate. I can remember looking through the letterbox and the brand-new windows, and the eery silence of a completely empty house staring back at me. The police couldn't find her, and apparently not one of her friends or family members knew where she was or anything about what was happening. She wasn't at Mr Robertson's house when we drove past. And no one was home when we knocked. Even though the curtains twitched with intrigue. She had just fallen into the abyss. Lucky her.

So just like that we were my dad's. He had won the war. And while we were camped out at my granny's house, him leaving us there so he could maintain the illusion of his real life, triumphant, chest puffed up with magnificence and grandeur he returned to us. He was very, very pleased with himself. Except he hadn't expected to have to give up quite so much. Trading in his newest child in a two-for-one deal. It was us or them, his girlfriend of seven years had told him. She had been by his side the whole time, pompously judging my mother's actions with disdain. How could anyone stop a child from seeing their father? What kind of person would do such a thing?

Collateral damage, they call it. She was shocked by his response, by the obligatory position he had placed himself in, chasing his win. And he was shocking in his management of it all.

We, apparently, in our need for parents, had ruined his life. And didn't we know it. Reminding us, each and every time we stepped out of line. Or asked for cake at the supermarket. He was miserable because of us. We were ungrateful, spoilt little shits and needed to wake up and smell the coffee. How could we be playing, enjoying life? When his was over? And for what? For two useless children and a litany of one-night stands.

He wasn't around much after the initial period. Preferring the comfort of drink and clubs and throwaway women. We dutifully made dinner for his return and ironed his going-out clothes and sat mummified in front of the Sky Box every night. We managed our own bedtime routine and got ourselves up for school, and I lost all my teeth in the process. How novel not to have to clean them! Or do homework. Or go to sleep before 1:00 a.m. Or go to school at all.

School was something that I avoided like the plague. My only friend from year seven had upgraded to a better school. And her real friends, no doubt. And I was again skulking the playground. So, given I finally had a choice to run or to stay, I left school behind for the comforting isolation of riding the tube. Sometimes it felt for days on end. I was unwanted. Discarded. Like a ragged teddy. Frayed around the edges from overuse. Lost and long forgotten. Weathered and dirty, waiting patiently on the park bench for someone to reclaim me. To claim me. Motionless. Unable to move, or talk, think or reach out for love. Reach out for hope. No mum. No dad. No friends. No community. In despair. Shell-shocked from it all.

The first we had heard of my mother's existence was upon receipt of a postcard. Two weeks after she sold our house from under us. Beautifully penned from the holiday we were supposed to be on. She wished we were there. I guess she is where I get my love of words. My command of the English language.

And where my mother is a pro of prose, my father's speciality was maths, and this is undoubtably where I get my calculating nature. Him meticulously counting the cards held close to his chest. And all the money he stole from the charity pots. This, no doubt, where I developed my thirst for the analysis of it all.

When he was home, we spoke at length. Don't just go with what you feel, Fran. Look from every possible angle and then decide what is right, Fran. Do the right thing, Fran. Even if it turns out to be the wrong thing. Good advice. When you have no idea how you actually feel. The fallout of PTSD, I suppose. And disorders can last a lifetime. No wonder I have never felt able to move forward. Or understand myself. Or go with my heart. Or command any self-respect.

I get it though. It was preferable for him. To manage life in this way. It offers control in a scary world. And control was my father's antidote. Self-medicating his way through life by keeping himself and everyone else and his feelings and his heart in place. Carefully constructed partitions to ensure that he never needed to feel the hurt of his childhood. Carefully constructed barriers. Around himself and the outside world.

He was still traumatised. Stressed. Disordered. Post childhood. What do you expect when your mother leaves you, age four, for another country. Another life. Whisked away in alluring promises of the wind rush. And sends for her new husband before you. And then God kills your grandmother and your only comfort, and your father's new wife replaces you with a new child as soon as she can. So you go to the only place where there is anyone who has any responsibility, any liability for you. Traveling days. Alone and scared on the banana boat to England. Only to be beaten and disregarded when you finally arrive. Luggage in hand. Heart in mouth. To find the man who was preferential to you has found another woman, another family, who is preferential to him. And a mother who was too young to have birthed you, bitter and vengeful. And you're the reason.

So you work. You work hard. To gain favour. Age twelve and sewing and stitching. Your fingers and your heart hardened, covered in calluses. Shoes used as airborne projectiles whenever your true feelings spill out. Slowly falling into crime and gambling to find escape. And eventually becoming maid and servant to your disabled mother. Dutifully attending every Wednesday to cook up home food. And be told you're a donkey. And cussed out. And thrown out. Only to return. Dutifully waiting on the payout that never comes. Your mum too smally island mentality to have realised she was signing away the use of her spine to the doctor's experiments.

He tried to talk to me about it once. Before he died. Lying in his hospital bed and reassessing his life. I tried to be gracious and explain things simply. "You always create hurdles for people to climb over to prove their love, Dad. But it just pushes us all away. I understand you and forgive you. I love you." I'm glad he gave me the gift of wisdom in times of need.

Apparently, though, his new wife and her daughters didn't like this level of self-introspection. So I got attacked next to his hospital bed as he looked on. Completely disabled by the powerlessness of the situation he had landed himself in. It honestly broke my heart. Watching him. Watching on. Knowing he had facilitated this through his own fucked-up need for control.

Because even I understand the trauma. The pain he went through. And how he needed, he really needed, the control. Without it, anything could happen. How he never really felt comfortable in his own skin. So had to use reasoning and analysis and intellect to figure everything out. Unlocking those dormant feelings would be way too unconstrained. He would be unrestrained. And we couldn't have that. So bullying and browbeating his children and his loved ones into submission was the way to go. My way or the highway.

He was always putting his foot down. On my neck. Metaphorically choking the life out of me. I can remember being twelve, thirteen, fourteen, covered with spit during his two-hour rants. Venom spewing from his lips. Aggression and hate for us so close I could smell it on his breath. But the problem is, that approach only works for so long. When someone has nowhere else to go. And eventually, the open highway starts to look appealing.

So at the age of fourteen, just after my shameful doorstep sexual assault – the one I was ultimately responsible for because I rolled up my school skirt above knee height – I took the rest of our pilfered stack. Stacked up in pound coins in the glass cabinet and took to the highway. It only took me as far as my mother's house.

We had had only sporadic contact. All of us still reeling from our first, post-move, encounter. And the emaciated frame of my mother. And her dark eyes and even darker behaviour. Of the treatment of my once loving family towards us and my "nigger father". Of our coached demands for our 66 (.6) percent of the household goods. Two-thirds into 100 percent. Divide the hundred by three and times by two. 66.6. My dad was gracious with the 0.6.

And how my mum threw me backwards into a table despite her skinny frame. And pierced my thigh with her nails so deep that I still have a scar to this day, on the ride to our house to get our rightly deserved things. And how she had given away all of our toys to Thomas Robertson's niece and nephew. And how all my clothes were gone. And how there was nothing of our life with her left. And how now there is nothing left of my spinal processor, my muscles now forever tight and strained to compensate for the loss. Much like the rest of me.

So, fourteen and a runaway, Dad came to claim me back. Screaming that I would never see him again if I didn't get in the car. Right now, Francisca. He was putting his foot down again, but I didn't care anymore.

Thomas was still there. And still fucked up. Something happened with the iron. And my mum's arm. But I'm not sure. I am sure that the shattered plate with my Indian takeaway is still somewhere in the back garden though. Apparently, the phone was not for conversing. It was for sending messages. And that shouldn't take more than two minutes. So you can imagine Thomas's indignation returning to a teenage girl who had been on the phone for thirty whole minutes. And who had condoned this?

After my mum had argued her position as my mother and an equal part of this household and ordered Indian for us as an alternative to wearily preparing food, he ripped the phone from its perch. And the phone cable from the wall. And when it arrived, locked us in the kitchen. Him a human barricade. And when we finally were allowed out, threw my plate, food, fork and all into the garden. To teach us a lesson. My mum sat quietly contained throughout. I screamed useless profanities at him. Cursing him and his life. Then we all went to bed, some of us empty tummied, and never spoke of it again.

She didn't finally get rid of him until he woke me up in a seething rage. The day of my first GCSE. Smashing my stereo to pieces. Apparently, the alarm was too loud for his liking. Me and my mum went on the Venice holiday he had prepared for that portion of the cycle. And she was resolute. He was back within two years. I didn't care much anymore because I was eighteen and living elsewhere. I gave him my best Godfather-style warning. He stayed long enough to break my mum's heart again and then return to the other woman he had had all along. And the child he had never wanted with her. And I achieved three A's and a catalogue of other decent marks in my GCSEs anyway. So fuck him.

So I guess when it comes down to it, we're all just victims. Of circumstance and one another's pain. We're all sinners. No one's sin is worse than another's. There's no wonder that I ever felt worthy. Before or after my salvation. There's no wonder that it was so easy to fall back into fear and despair. Into the default of being pitiful. Unlovable. Unsavable. To believe that the momentary glance of contentment was all I was due. Merely glimpsing a life and a feeling that others were destined for. But not me.

Because the feeling of worthiness is something that is passed down through the ages. Through the blood. Because bliss is not a constant state. Not until we go up there. Back to Him. But the knowing of worth that was given to you before you were a concept in your mother' womb – that you are worthy because God put you here. And he loves you. And through this you can ultimately have belief in yourself and your own worth. The knowing of this means you have to put behind you all the pain of the past and everything that every person has ever inflicted on you. And be like Him. Like Jesus. Kind. Compassionate. Gentle. Merciful. Peacekeeping. Pure of heart.

Don't judge that you be judged. He truly is the narrow way, and that takes serious faith. Not just the sometimes-throwaway faith that comes hand in hand with the doctrines of a religion. But unfettered belief that you are always on the right path. That all roads lead to Him. Without reassurance. Without understanding. Without any true awareness of the destination. Because this is my journey. And everyone has their own. And faith in one another is vital to true salvation. Hardened, steadfast faith in you and everyone around you. To be able to see all as God does. Worthy. Complete. And deserved of love. Deserved of salvation, of the covenant God wrote for you before you were born. Saved, loved, redeemed and His.

5 July 2020

I start by asking God to save me. I plead with Him like a frightened child on their first day of school. I pray three, sometimes four times a day. I meditate. On Jesus. On God. On power. On autonomy. And I listen. For Him. I start educating myself on evil spirits, temptation, the devil. I pray each night and every morning for protection. I pray to remove negative spirits. I sing in praise. And I listen. For Him.

I seek out people who can help and guide me. I talk to other believers. I find the help I need, and I begin to arm myself against the enemy. And I listen. For Him.

The messages from God come thick and fast, and my power strengthens.

Some days I am love. Merrily searching for the rot and listening for the whispers and finding nothing. Some days I wake in agony. Devastated by some unseen bereavement. And on these days, I fight back. Repeating over and over that it is I who has the authority. I who holds the power. I who makes the commandments. God gave me this. As well as the power of Jesus' name.

And when this doesn't work, I think of Jesus. Who He is. What He did for me. For all of us. His perfection. His love. His kindness, His mercy, and it floods my soul with love. It warms my heart, and I no longer feel compelled to doubt. To sadness. Or to evil.

I often ask the Holy Spirit to enter me and fill me with light. I ask Jesus to lie with me in those waking hours of darkness. And I fear and ask God to remind me of the strength and the power I have. They never fail me. When I need them. Whenever I ask for them, they appear to me. In thought. In feeling. And in spirit.

Irrespective of the level of severity. I find, every day, there is need to fight. A need to battle on. Sometimes the battle is won quickly, and sometimes it rages on, but eventually. We. Are. Always. Victorious.

This only enrages the enemy. As he returns. Time after time. To try and retake me. He knows he is losing. Ultimately. He has lost. But he won't give up without a fight. Hoping against hope that he will catch me when I am weak and vulnerable. Catch me slipping.

But I learn to listen. To my self. To my voice. To my body and my soul. And I begin, quickly, to be able to distinguish me from him. Me from them. Me from it. And through this, I am able to hear and overcome it easily. Sometimes I talk to it directly. I tell it how pathetic it is. How I despise it and everything it stands for. How I will never, ever again be ruled by its hatred. By sin. I tell it that I am now in charge. I rule here. I compel. I control. I command.

But often I simply ignore it. It's not worthy of my time, my anger or my hatred. As it loves when I am compromised by hate. Even if it's for the enemy itself. I ignore it. Not even giving its pathetic attempts any attention. And laughing in my head at the futility of its pitiful efforts. Laughing at how helpful it has become in my redemption. It is almost comical. The weapons it has at its disposal.

The power of suggestion.

Like nothing more than a second-rate magician using the art of distraction to steal your soul from right under your nose. Only to have to return it once the jig is up.

There is, I learn, a distinct difference between being possessed and oppressed.

And knowing your own infinite power. Knowing the battle starts and ends in your own mind. And knowing His omnipotent, omnipresence in your fight. That you have Him on your squad. Powers you on in the war. Even now as I write, I am aware of the battle I face today, slightly more alight with the rumblings of fear, of irritation, of anger than the days prior.

Because the whisperings never stop. It never stops trying. But it is our job, our duty. To ourselves and to God to be a soldier, a warrior in this war. Immovable. In our faith. In ourselves. In our strength. And this is only possible through standing with Jesus.

So say no.

Say, "I deny you".

Say, "I rebuke you".

Command it to leave.

Do not give in.

Do not succumb.

Fight on.

Fight on.

What if, Five

WHAT IF, 5) **IT DIDN'T TAKE AN EXORCISM TO WAKE YOU UP? IF THE REAL BATTLE WASN'T OUT THERE, BUT IN HERE? WHAT IF PATIENCE, DISCERNMENT, UNDERSTANDING AND COMPASSION, FAITH IN YOU AND EVERYONE AROUND YOU AND LOVE, REAL, TRUE LOVE, WERE THE ARMOUR NEEDED TO BE FORGED IN THIS BATTLE? WHAT IF YOU REALISED YOU HAD AN ALLY SO POWERFUL YOU COULD WIPE OUT THE ENEMY WITH A FLICK OF YOUR FINGER, IF ONLY YOU COULD BECOME CLEAR WHO THE ENEMY TRULY WAS?**

WHAT IF YOU DRAGGED BACK THE VEIL TO REVEAL THAT GOOD AND EVIL ACTUALLY EXISTED?
WHAT IF YOU WOKE UP AND REALISED WHO'S SIDE YOUR IGNORANCE HAD CHOSEN FOR YOU?

WOULD YOU CHOOSE AGAIN?

My dad always told us it was our right to know everything that happened in court and everything my mum said to the judge. I was probably seven when I first heard the term *affidavit*. What was that? Well, apparently it was important, because it made my mum a liar.

So by the time I was twelve and situated at my father's. After all the fanfare. After all the drama and commotion. After the shift. So, by the time I was twelve, I was well versed with what a court document looked like. He told me that he had left it out, intentionally for me to read. You never knew with my dad. He was such a fantasist. He was such a controllist. Even if he didn't mean to do it, he would never admit it. He was always masterful. In each juncture. In each moment. In each mistake. Because he never made mistakes. So maybe he did or maybe he didn't. All I know is that it was read.

Stories about me. Stories about my life. Stories about my past. My mum, my dad and my heresy. She refused to see us at the court, when it finally came time to give evidence. Fourteen and dressed in my best power suit. I don't think she wanted to look me in the eye and call me a child molester. So me and my big bro walked the streets, and my dad didn't have any contact with my little sister after that day. She still thinks she was a child of sexual abuse.

I don't know what I was a child of. I've wrestled so many days with it. Laid awake so many nights with it. Toying with the possibility that it could be true. And the nightmares didn't help. Or my dad's cruel and dismissive ways. Or reading about it in an affidavit. A chicken barely sprung. But apparently capable of heinous crimes.

It was the only time he really, actually stood up for us. The only time he made the decision to put us first. And sacrificed something for it. The only time he said no, I will not allow someone, anyone, to treat you poorly, for my own gain.

Because he knew it wasn't right. To allow his child to be called a paedophile. Not because he had pissed off this specific woman with his choices. Because he didn't really have a choice once my mum sold our house from under us. But maybe because of all the women he had pissed off beforehand and all the pissed-off women to come. To have driven someone to such anger that they would do that to you. To your child. And he couldn't let me take the fall for it. Not this time.

By the time I was nineteen he had already staggered his way through a corridor of women. A new and sublime option behind each closed door. Sue was nice. I liked her. Despite being introduced the night before the family holiday she and her daughter were due to accompany us on. I wish she had stuck around. Even if her daughter was a terrible influence. Keeping me out late, bunking me off school, taking me to boys' houses, having sex in the other room and giving me my first skud to smoke, aged twelve. But he could never say he loved her. And apparently that was the deal from the beginning. She just couldn't stick to it. So it became a dealbreaker.

My first proper Christmas with Josh was at his new woman's house. The first one didn't really count, given he was in a Perspex box and I was back home, looking for something I had lost. Christmas had been strange and estranged before that. Given he had disowned me for the past three years. I had tried to call him once. On Christmas day. To wish him a Merry Christmas. He had clarified there was nothing else, and hung up. Christmas has become a strange affair in my household. I can't remember the last time I spent it with either parent. And being with them on such a special day feels like having an affair. Disloyal to myself and to people who care for and accept me.

I used to make individualised placemats for our guests when I was younger. I would set the table lovingly and meticulously and help my mum in any way I could. Even when she was flustered and screaming at us because everything was coming together swimmingly. I would cut the tags for my gifts from last year's Christmas cards, lovingly kept and carefully reused. I would tenderly fold my wrapping paper after opening gifts, a ritual left over from the Thomas Robertson days, and we would patiently and eagerly watch one another open one gift at a time.

I don't think there were placemats the year I was asked to leave though. I don't think we had gotten to that point yet. We had only just woken up really. And, yes, Josh was crying and needed changing. But my friend was crying and needed me. I mean, it's not every year that you enter Christmas Day having been assaulted, pushed around, shoved against a wall. Had a gun put in your face. If only I had stayed, maybe things would have gone differently. But Karin can't help but win pool. She's a national champion, after all. Even if it insults your fragile male ego.

My mum was denigrating me. She liked to do that. Any time I didn't do what she wanted me to. And she liked to hold my need for support and a break from a disabled child over my head. And if I didn't like what she said, what she did, how she did it or what her expectations were, I could fuck off. Essentially. Going out consisted of a ritual designed and enforced by her, put him to sleep, stay, wait, return, wake him up. Mother would provide the vessel in which he stayed. And berate me if he woke up in the middle of the night. And remind me to be grateful and contrite. And point her bony finger at me through gritted teeth if I didn't.

And this time was no different. She was livid that I wasn't doing as I was told. Incensed that I would dare to defy her. When she knew best. His leg isn't going to fall off because he isn't changed for ten minutes, mum. That went down like a lead balloon. And my friend needs me; it's serious. And I was going down with it.

And the details didn't save me. It was the first time I was challenging her rule, after such benevolence on her part. And I didn't quite know how to do it. So I appealed to her better nature. Her compassion. Her humanity. Her femininity.

Well, apparently, if you go to places like that, with people like that, what do you expect? We swiftly ascertained that she meant black people and that, furthermore, she was extremely affronted when I called her a racist. So much so that she left me to walk the hour-long journey home with the pushchair as my only crutch.

This Christmas was different though. With this strange new family. And I didn't like their rituals. I didn't like the grotesque mound of presents under the tree. I didn't like the fact that they all feasted on wrapping paper, ripping to shreds the labour someone had made, in a frenzy of greed and wide-eyed, glinting, menacing grins. I didn't like that you didn't even know who got what and no one said thanks properly. And I certainly didn't like the ritual of my father lying to another woman and asking me to cover it up.

No, I certainly would not tell her you were with me yesterday. And if she asks, I will impart the truth. So you had better hope she's not particularly inquisitive. I was the one though. Through my drive for morality and goodness. Or more like my desire to make things OK and be seen as good and wholesome, and clever and honourable. I was the one who told him to choose. Told him to be honest for once. Reminded him of his own mortality and how lonely eighty could be. I was the one who set it in stone. And what a fucking error that was.

My dad once told me that he had chosen Toni because of her lack of experience. Because she had only been with one man and he thought she would be more malleable to his rule. To his way of doing things. To his needs. As the man of the house. But a lack of partners does not mean a lack of experience. And what Toni had experienced was cruelty and abuse and the desperation of needing, above your own life, to stay, for the sake of her children. And she was not malleable. She was not timid; she was not retiring or fainthearted. She was a bully. Having been bullied and finally finding her feet. Her mouth. Her arms. Her fists. This the only language of love she really knew.

The first time he facilitated it, Josh was nearly three. Josh's dad had opted out prebirth, and his grandmother had told me to abort. So it was novel that they were having some contact. That they had made the decision to commit to Josh – after I pursued his father on the streets of Catford and offered him another choice. Either way, they wanted to take him to America. And I was game. I had never, in his or my life, had more than a few hours away from my son. And I was desperate.

Following the requests for evidence of return flights and following the humiliation of requests for written confirmation they would bring him home, they still came. Dad and Toni. To tell me that they wouldn't pay for my flights if Josh got sick in the US. And he would die without me. Scared and alone. And hating his mother. And I would have to live with it. And to tell me that I was selfish and childish and immature and selfish. And to remind me what my role as a mother was. And that I wasn't meeting it. And to meet Tara, just to make sure she was really going to bring him home. And eventually remind her that she had wanted to kill him and that she was a cunt.

And having made no progress. Progressed to inform me that I was no longer invited to their wedding. As Toni didn't want pieces of shit like me walking down the aisle behind her. And progressed the inquisition onto my mother's house and into a nearby pub. And pressed me into a corner. Three on one. Well one and half if you include Josh, who was happily ignorant to it all. So maybe just one of us then.

I sat silently while they berated me and scolded me and cursed me and my decisions. And I crouched silently in the tall grass of the pub garden. Pretending to my son that it was such a fun game. My dad's inference that he would call the police and social services on me if I allowed Josh to go, and ruin my life and my career, and make sure I never saw my son again ringing in my ears. If I'm honest, I was delighted and marginally relieved at the end of the two weeks, and Josh was returned safely to me.

We didn't talk much after that. Me and any of them. The first I heard from the tribe was a call from my stepsister, on the day of my dad's wedding. Telling me it wasn't right. That I should be there. That we were family.

So I confided in her that it had been a difficult day. My crazed downstairs neighbour, who liked to blast music in the early hours, once I'd gotten my toddler back to sleep. And smear my car with acid. And report me to the housing office for smoking crack and running a brothel, myself being the only gainful employee. And write fourteen-page letters about my sexual exploits. And ask me if I could get her weed from anywhere. My crazed downstairs neighbour had finally had all my things removed. Despite there being very little evidence of any noise pollution – other than that I was young and brown and immoral. And she was white and middle class. And sociopathic.

Having confided my situation, I promptly received a phone call from my mother. To remind me that the PC was technically hers and to inform me that if I didn't get it back, I would, of course, owe her. And that she was not happy. Not impressed, disappointed, really. Happy wedding day to you dad. Thank you for letting us share in your special day. Here's to a lifetime of happiness and love.

I was pretty accustomed to being disowned, so the absence of my father in my life for a few years, every few years, was unremarkable. When we did speak, he offered pearls of wisdom and flickers of true, unreserved and unabated love. He was my confidant, and I genuinely treasured our time together. And Toni was helpful and caring in her own way. She thought about the kids. She bought the presents. And she paid the mortgage for the house my dad lived in. And, of course, graciously allowed him to stay there. But that's what happens when you spend your children's university inheritance on a loose lifestyle and loose women and then invest all of your money into a property that is not even part owned by you. That's what happens when you don't want to declare your income so that you can continue living off the state. Compromises, I guess.

And they both helped me move. Several times. And Toni even had pity for me when my mum refused to wait for me to get Callum's cot to her house, so he had somewhere to sleep for the night, my house move somewhat delayed after being thrown down a flight of stairs by his dad. She had a hair appointment. And Toni was angry when I was beaten up and tear stained when I nearly died in labour. So there was emotion, no doubt. But there was always a catch.

A rule of engagement, of being with them, that I couldn't quite catch hold of. I don't remember now all the times Toni was abusive to me. Or abusive to my dad. All the times he stood silently by. Complicit at best and goading at worst in my abuse. But I remember having to swallow my pride a lot. Like dry bread. Swallow my voice and swallow my tongue. For the sake of my father. This never more pertinent than when his kidneys failed, and he had nothing and no one else to rely on but her.

She called him a nigger once. In the heat of an argument, but still. It's not the sort of thing that just slips out. Or that you can shove back in. He pleaded to stay with me after that. To call social services. To help. I did all I could and called with instruction, but he was unwilling to report her, and ultimately unwilling to give up his lifestyle – he had it cushty. Other than the racial abuse.

She put her hands on me multiple times. And multiple times I suffered the indignity of not fighting back. Of standing, clenched fists and motionless. The only signal that I was alive the bead of sweat caressing my face. And the slight twitch in my mouth. Disgust yearning to spill out. Two finger digs to the head. Bitch, whore, cunt in her mouth. Bile in her stomach for me. And my dad, smaller and paler as the years went on, watching on in horror in the moment. Then consoling himself with platitudes about my attitude outside of it. About Courtney's attitude, him daring to suggest that Toni's aggressive behaviour might signal, despite her denials, that she was not, in fact, OK.

She messaged me to tell me what a selfish bitch I was once. And that she hoped I would die. That I likely worshipped the devil, and that I should have been aborted. That my younger sister was a more likely choice for daughter of the year. And she had been missing since the '90s. She was struggling with caring for my dad full time. I wanted to help, but he refused to hear from me, given I was not fully supportive of his decision to stay with a racist bully and had instructed me to go through his wife for a face-to-face appointment. I politely declined. But left my metaphorical door open for him, for any future meetings.

Nevertheless, I did dutifully travel the 220 miles to see him when he had his first – or was it second or third? – stroke. Even though he confessed, in his foggy state, that if he had known this was the contract, he would never have had me. And I sat and guided him through the funk of his depression, reminding him of the wonders of life and the power of gratitude. And finally got him to start the crossword puzzles his brain had always relished.

And again, I covered the distance. When he had his cardiac arrest and was left to bleed out in his ward. I even tried to give advice about possible litigation. Given the hospital's grave negligence.

The final time, I was, as always, trying my hardest to stay out of it. But she didn't like my dad's newfound introspection. She didn't like that he was making some peace with his behaviour. She didn't like that he was looking at himself. And might likely start to look at her too. And she certainly didn't like that he wanted the beep-beep machine to stop, if only for a while. Or that he called her out for aggressing him, because she didn't agree. Didn't condone it. Called her out for aggressing him, right there in the hospital. And for every time at home.

And she tried everything. To get me to bite. But I was busy with Candy Crush. And crushing her implicit attacks. Until the attack was no longer implicit and the rage overtook me and I embarrassed myself and my dignity in front of the nursing staff.

So she warned my dad against me. Reminded him who I was, who she was, who had been there for him. And her daughter politely questioned where he might go, once he was released. I tried to help him. I tried to get him out. I tried to do what he asked. But he was too selfish. And I was too selfish. I wasn't willing to put myself through any more pain. Or be told I was useless. Or be screamed at down the phone. Or woken in the middle of the night.

I didn't see him for months after that. I didn't know. I didn't see the signs. So I missed the part where he fell into madness and didn't have to sit by and watch as he lost all sense of reality. But I guess that's what you miss when you're swept up in yourself and your own disdain. Your own dislike and distrust for others. When you're not able to see past the end of your own pain. To the beauty that would unfold if you could be beautiful. In your heart and your actions.

When I finally went to see him, I silently broke as he called me mummy and tried to drink his toast, asked to come with me and called me his painful daughter. And I rejoiced when he joined in with me, singing my year-six Christmas solo. And I didn't even mention anything about it when he miraculously woke up. Three days after my visit. And eight months after he was lost to us all. I supported Toni to have her moment. Her rightful pride. Her rightful place.

Because when it comes down to it. I never wanted to be hateful. That came much later. I think I always understood that fighting back was not a tool at my disposal. I was too shy and too meek and too cowardly. I never have had the strength for assertiveness, so much of the time I submitted and allowed things to happen. And blamed others and complained about my position. Victimised by it all.

Be more assertive, the world says. And what is assertive anyway? The having and the showing of a forceful personality? Hailed in today's society. The assertive woman, formidable in her attributes. Fearless in her conquests. But fighting back was never a tool at my disposal. Neither was love. And this is why the stalemate of my victimised position persisted. I heard once that if there are things in life that persist, even when you say you don't want them to. Then really you do. Really you are gaining something from it. Despite losing something in the payoff.

I'd like to think that it was simply my kind and compassionate nature that stopped me from standing up for myself all those years. Against all of them. My mum, my dad, my associates. My friends, cousins, stepdads, stepmums and stepsiblings. My children's fathers. Their parents. All the men. All the partners. Courtney. All of them. But it wasn't. It was my shameful desire to be liked. To be accepted. To be victim. But more importantly, it was my complete lack of awareness of how to love.

Because it was so much easier. So much easier when they were mean. And then I was mean. I had the excuse. A wonderful exemption in my hands, opened up in offering. Yet to whom? I could be the willing victim of their hurt and their pain and be hurtful and painful in response. How much easier it was when I didn't need to try, when I didn't need to be better. I could be worse. The same. Powerful in condemnation. Of others. Of myself. And beautifully powerless to it, all at once.

I see them. All of it. I see their pain, their anguish. It's written all over their hurt faces. And their hurtful words. Their hateful actions and every piece of power they gained at my expense. And I understand that for the most part, it's not even them. It's evil incarnate. It's the pain of their past and the fear of their future, hurtling towards them. With no other way out than through.

And I do see me. All of it. I see my pain, my anguish. It's written all over my hurt face. And my hurtful words. My hateful actions and every piece of power I gained at their expense. And I understand that for the most part, it's not even me. It's evil incarnate. It's the pain of my past and the fear of my future, hurtling towards me. With no other way out than through.

Because there are forces beyond our recognition. At the periphery of our awareness. That thing that we can't quite see, can't quite catch. Egging us on. When we know we shouldn't, when we don't even want to. A small yet determined voice just behind our ear. Whispering. Compelling. It darkens our faces and our hearts, only momentarily. But for long enough that eventually we see nothing but injury. Injured from the ruin of it all. And injuring others just to get by. It's just too tempting to take all that pain, ball it up into a cacophony of grief and hurtle it at others. Hadouken. And fight!

So do we sit? Victimised and forlorn? In a meditative state that cannot be penetrated by the outside? Do we react? Do we respond and retaliate? Do we fight back? How do we let it be? How can we? We are helpless, so how do we help? How do we relieve ourselves and others? How does any of it relieve us from a cylinder of hurt and hurting? An ornate chamber within which we countermand our responsibility to love. Like a love-struck Henry. On his eighth wife.

But I know now that fighting back doesn't consist of meeting that anger where it lives. Evilness in people is more easily seen when you push back. It awakes it. It invokes it. It's where it lives, seeping from one person to the next. Fighting back with snarky comments and equal disdain. Or vengeful anger, this only fuels the fires of hell.

But you can push back. You should push back. Not against the people, though, not against the individual and their individual pain. But against the evil itself. Jesus loved those who persecuted him. Even in the midst of it. He hung on that cross, telling each and every one of us that he loved us. That he was doing it for us. Even when they jeered. When they sneered. When they turned their backs and called for a thief to be set free. He never allowed who we were to change his love for us. And while he hanged there, he never hung us for it.

It is therefore our job to love, even when it's hard. Even when it hurts. And the world will love us for doing so. Love is all enduring. All encompassing. All consuming. But being steadfast in love does not mean hitching your wagon to one person and weathering the storm, twisted wood, beaten and bowed throughout the years. Colour-faded faces, weathered from the storm. Love endures when we choose, *we* choose. To never, ever allow the pain of others, inflicted greedily and mercilessly on us, change what we are. Who we are. To never bite back. But to fight back.

Because it is only through this level of love, this unabated, unfettered, unsoiled, unsullied love. This ultimate kindness, that He can work through us and touch others. And this is the true power of Christ. This is the true power of faith, and love, and man and God. This is who we are in His image. This is how we love others as we love ourselves. Walk a mile in my shoes, and you will forgive me. Walk a meter in my shoes, and you will know me. And to know me is to love me. And to love me is to forgive me. To let it go. To declare brazenly: I owe you nothing. And you owe me nothing. But that we owe God. Our lives. Our hearts. The very essence of love. The rights to every trial overcome and every battle won. The thanks for each lesson learned. Him carefully moulding our lives and our hearts and minds through the adversities we face. And how much easier it is to overcome these atrocities, these affronts, with love pouring from our hearts. Touching each person, each situation, each tribulation we face.

I wish I was better. Better at this. At being kind even when I am crying out in pain. I wish I could love even when it hurts me. I wish I could forgive more easily and reach a shaking hand out to those I despise. And I know despise me. In those moments, I wish I could be better. Do better. Love better. And I don't excuse it. I don't excuse myself, my behaviour or my scorn.

And this is why God continues to test and to teach me. Like a father, watching on as his child makes the same mistakes, over and over. Knowing that He could save me, He could pick me up and deposit me somewhere else. Only for me to do the same thing. And how painful it must be. It is. To watch me in anguish, in pain. Hurting myself and others along the way. But like the father I never really had, He sacrifices His own need for release, for sanctification, to allow us to suffer for our own good. And we hate Him. We berate Him. We chastise Him for it. We call out to Him in venomous anger. "Why have You forsaken me? Why did You do this to me, God? Why did you allow this to happen?" We blame Him and all those around us for our own pain and misery, like little children, sulking and crying over our own shitty choices.

Because I am not a victim. I have hurt as much as I have been hurt. I am no better than anyone I dislike, anyone I have offered up for sacrifice in this book. Teaching them a lesson, like I don't have my own. And all these lessons. Through all these people. All these trials and tribulations. They are building me to be the person I am supposed to be. The person God made me. They are driving a resilience into me that is far beyond the need to resist.

Because God's armour is not made of metal or iron, and His weapons do not have spikes or blades. And resistance is futile. All we truly have at our disposal is our free will. That beautiful gift given to us all. And where do we choose to align our will, with good or bad, kindness or revenge, God or evil? Because through this choice, which is ours alone, we gain the weapons of the camp. Do we choose the belt of truth, the breastplate of righteousness, the shield of faith and the helmet of salvation? Or the intoxicating power found in blame and hate and harm?

Because only with these weapons can we fight. Against those in the flesh and those in the spirit. Against the spiritual forces of wickedness. Forces that compel others through their pain and sorrow to hate and anger. In the hope that you, too, will succumb to bitterness and rage and the whole world will eventually bend and kneel to rage and vengefulness. Hating each other and hating God and loving evil as the only catharsis for the pain of it all.

So love.

Love hard.

Even when it hurts.

Even when you feel like you can't. You shouldn't. You won't.

Fight on. In truth.

Fight on. In righteousness.

Fight on. In faith.

Fight on for your salvation. For the salvation of others.

Fight on. Fight on.

13 July 2020

The first message comes in a roundabout kind of way. Like most do. I've been living in fear for about a week now, and nothing I do seems to work. To shift it, the fear. My body is buzzing. Electrified with it. And I feel weak, tired, worn out. Courtney and I won't say it out loud, but we know we are being punished. We know our wrongs, our sins have allowed evil back into me. He blames me. I can see it on his face. And he hates himself for it. I keep referring to it as 'the devil'. I keep talking about the enemy. How I hate him. And hate him and hate him. Courtney can't understand it. It's irritating him. My whole state of being is irritating him. "The Bible never calls him the devil", he interjects on one occasion. He spits. Thrown out like an invitation. A polite and purposeful challenge. Like a slap to the face with a wayward glove. I'm banging on about how much power the enemy has, how scared I am. Courtney can recall something. Something or other about Jesus speaking to Lucifer in the desert. We look it up. Poised for some lyrics to fight this evil. To strip it of its power. To face the next round.

But what we get instead is a message. Offering reassurance and solace in a lost time. Something that immediately causes us both to release breath we hadn't even realised we were holding. Something that allows us to admit. To ourselves and each other. Finally. Just how petrified we are.

It is often, the video says, that the enemy comes to torment you. To try and reclaim you. After your most significant spiritual experience.

We sit in silent awe.

At the feeling this sentence alone brings. At the complete random nature of our search. And the completely unrelated agenda that motivated it.

But mainly, how this message pierces through as the only thing that needed to be heard. Like a bullet cutting through the fog of gunpowder all around us. So straight. So strong. So precise that you can look through the break it leaves in its wake. The eye of its very own storm. Heading straight for you. Completely unexpected and completely on target. Dead centre at your heart.

This sparks the beginning. Of my veiled counsel. Coming from a mouth that could not be seen, but would be heard. If I listen closely enough. God comes to me in my dreams. "The Sermon on the Mount", he whispers. Like an instruction, a mission. Almost lost in the memories of my dreams. A phrase I haven't heard in decades. A thing long forgotten. Since Sunday school and a life I can barely remember more than the dreams of last night. But this message. This message endures. Throughout the night. I take it into each new dream. Each semiconscious waking moment. Holding on to until I awake. Sun up and my message clear in the light of the new day.

When I finally get around to reading it, I don't really understand. So I delve deeper. And am finally punctured by the message sent for me. It's OK. You're OK. You are good. You are gentle. You are merciful, pure of heart, a peacemaker. Fear not. Despite all you have been through. All you have done and all you regret, Jesus sees you. Jesus saved you. Jesus loves you. Be at peace and know that all Jesus wants from you, you have inside. I am flooded with relief in the midst of my sorrow and grief. My pain and guilt. My shame and anguish.

I am calmed and solaced in my waking hours. I am reassured that I am good and loved. And forgiven my discretions. I am the person Jesus speaks about. I have a soul and there is good in me. I am redeemable and have been redeemed. I do not need to worry. To wrestle with anxiety. I do not need to face each day in inner turmoil. I am exactly what God is looking for. And the evil I once felt. The evil I fear has returned cannot find a place here. It can't live in the light. Or make you die in darkness. Because you are all that is written here.

And I finally find solace in my sleep. Just as I finally succumb to the torment that I will again be tormented through the night. Finally stating my exhaustion and despair out loud. A prayer, sent at random, by a person I barely know. The exorcism lady, learning of my plight and wanting to help. With no clear understanding of how, or her significance in this journey. Timed to perfection.

And I am renewed and renewed in my reasons. And the reason for these harrowing experiences. Learning from multiple sources their own messages. Of my ministry for God. Of my purpose. Of my decree. I will write the book I have already penned. I will sing the praises I am already singing. Films speaking directly to me. As a message. To stay strong on my journey. Arm myself against the enemy. Understand my role as a soldier in the war in and around me.

And I find solace.

I begin speaking my story again. With God's encouragement. With his blessing it seems. And I am rewarded with the joy in others' eyes and more messages. Message upon message upon message.

I wake again. Another night of torture overcome. Psalm 63 on my lips. Recalling my call for a psalm of my own. Encouraged and inspired the day before by those I have encouraged and inspired. Yes. My soul does thirst for You. Yes. I do earnestly seek You. Yes. My mouth will praise You, when I remember you on my bed, when I think of you in the night watchers. And, yes. Those who seek my soul to destroy it will be given over to the power of the sword. Those who speak lies will be silenced.

Lyrics seek me out and find me. God orchestrating YouTube algorithms. Disc-jockeying me inspiration.

In times of fear:

> "I will send out an army to find you.
>
> In the middle of the darkest night.
>
> It's true. I will rescue you."
>
> Lauren Daigle, Rescue.

In times of weakness:

> "This will end like I want it to.
>
> I win.
>
> The enemy will have to lose.
>
> Again.
>
> See, I'm a different fighter now."
>
> Jonathan McReynolds, Cycles.

In times of uncertainty:

> "Not by might. Not by power.
>
> By Your spirit God.
>
> Send Your spirit God."
>
> Tasha Cobbs Leonard, Your Spirit.

In times of anguish, unrest and torment on my soul:

> "Every time there's hope, it seems to die
>
> And the voices all around me feed that lie.

Everything I see tells me to let go.

Yet it is well.

With my Soul."

Tori Kelly, Soul's Anthem.

And I sing. And I write. And I listen. And I hear.

So why is it then? That we always hear the voice of the enemy so loudly? Why does it infiltrate all our thoughts? Sending its own message. Of hate. Of scorn. Of fear and deception? Why is God's voice so quiet? Seemingly so easily drowned out?

Quite simply, it is because, when you are that close to someone.

To be heard.

You only need to whisper.

What if, Six

WHAT IF, 6) **IT DIDN'T TAKE AN EXORCISM TO WAKE YOU UP? IF RELIGION HADN'T BASTARDISED ITSELF FOR INFAMY AND A SHOT AT BEING ON THE FRONT COVER OF 'SELL-OUT MILLENNIALLY', LEGS SPREAD AS WIDE AS ITS OWN BOGUS, MALIGN SMILE? WHAT IF EVERYTHING WASN'T GLAMOURISED AND YOU WEREN'T LEFT STAR-STRUCK AND DESENSITISED BY IT ALL? WHAT IF THOSE WHO SOUGHT TO INTERFERE SHOWED THEIR TRUE FACES AND IT HORRIFIED YOU? WHAT IF BELIEF IN SOMETHING HIGHER THAN POLITICS, A-LISTERS AND INFLUENCERS INFLUENCED YOU AND YOU WERE ABLE TO HEAR, SEE AND FEEL THE MESSAGES ALL AROUND YOU?**

WHAT IF YOU TORE BACK THE VEIL TO REVEAL THAT GOOD AND EVIL ACTUALLY EXISTED? WHAT IF YOU WOKE UP AND REALISED WHO'S SIDE YOUR IGNORANCE HAD CHOSEN FOR YOU?

WOULD YOU CHOOSE AGAIN?

I think I was about seven or eight when I first heard the term *messages* being used in such a strange way. Thomas Robertson, and his Celtic ancestry, sending me to the shop to get messages. With a shopping list. A list of needs, demands, desires, commands. As dictated and instructed by my elders. Penned and passed over for my own benefit and the benefit of my family.

But alas, sometimes I got lost in the aisles. Confused about what was needed. And scared that I would return empty-handed or with the wrong message. Sometimes I took too long. Veered off path. Got distracted by shiny objects and fanciful treats, wishing I could have the messages I wanted. Sometimes I didn't return. Sideswiped by my friends and temptation along the road home. And by the time I did, my messages were unripe and out of date. Useless for their intended purpose. Sometimes fear struck me halfway and I ran. Away from an unseen entity. Stalking me in the bushes, watching me through the aisles, leaving half my messages behind, dropping what was left, in my desperation to get back home. Back to the safety of my loved ones.

I think I was about the same age when I decided that God wasn't real. Seven or eight and already convinced by my small, limited world concept that there was nothing more than what was in front of my face. Nothing worth trusting in, or sacrificing for. Already disillusioned and disenfranchised. Jaded with the world and life and wonder. But it wasn't until I was twelve and had relocated to East London that I officially stopped going to church. I still went through the rituals before that, unquestioning. But not of the constancy of God's love, or the need for redemption and mercy., or the so-called righteousness of the Bible – and the infallibility of the priest. But unquestioning of everything. I didn't believe. In my heart. So there was nothing to question, nothing to seek, nothing to ponder. I forgot most of my Sunday school lessons. Like I forgot most of my life school lessons.

And I silently and subconsciously raged against the Bible. And religion. And God for years. Hidden behind intellect and reason, rationale and pragmatism. Empirically brandishing God with my own limited and predefined label. For most of my adult life I disregarded and dismissed and sullied His name, His work and His word. I hated to believe that there was a God that put me here. That gave me – that made me – this. So I dissected and analysed the concept of religion. I laughed at those who sought and saw miracles. As fantasists. As romantics. As madmen. As people who were so unhappy, so disconnected, so desperate that they had to turn to fairy tales just to get by. Just to find meaning in their sad little lives. In their sad little lies. And I felt real sorrow, pity, pathos for them and all those who believed.

And how easily I justified and was justified in my beliefs. In my religious corroding and goading of religion. And all things godly. In a world that corrodes the mind and the freedom of thought and choices. Through the guise of freedom of choice. Of free will. In a world that promotes the simplicity of individualism. Of serving yourself and your needs. In a world that shouts out, "Who are you? Who do you want to be?" Labels you like cattle and then tells you it's independence, uniqueness, individuality. Empowerment and vitality. When it is the very thing that divides and subjugates us. Conquers us while we are busy staring at the label of our neighbour, our friend, our family with disgust and distrust. Trying to figure out the ingredients and whether we can tolerate them.

Imagine. Imagine a world that would allow an eight-year-old school child to draw comparisons between Nazi Germany and the Blair administration. Or the globalisation of vaccinations with the same mindless compliance that murdered an entire generation. Imagine a world where our children are encouraged to discuss these matters. Where conjecture matters. Where they are encouraged, pushed, forced even. To open their minds and engage in real, critical debate about the world they will grow into. Imagine a world where circle time is sacked off, or grown to encompass active discussion. Instead of those who think out of the box being chastised, patronised and diminished. Reproached and censored. Assured that such connotations are off topic and not for the classroom. Or reassured that our GCSEs mean something only if we offer their answer. In our words. Prewritten and prethought. Preordained.

Preordained. By whom then? Who has decided what we do and what we do not learn, how we do and how we do not think? And what is rewarded and what is not? And why?

In the Victorian times children were taught in rows, sat at desks, having to raise their hands and comply with the system in order to prepare them for the systematic, laborious monotony of factory work. How far we have come. Grown into a world that is no longer built upon, driven by, slavery. Where we all have a fair chance and an equal crack. And none of us are pacified and passive through our financed lifestyles. Our HP cars and our catalogued trainers. Secretly cataloguing our success and status. Comfortable enough to never really have to consider how uncomfortable we are. How enslaved we are. To trash TV. To news. To Marvel epics. To sipping coffee through tiny, nippled cups. To £3 meal deals and *Just-fucking-Eat©*. To consuming; everything that there is out there. To capitalism. To keeping the system moving. Cogs in a wheel. So used to the constant background noise of life, and others telling us what to wear and what to listen to and what to eat and where to go and what to think that we can't eat and think and listen for ourselves. We can't hear anything else. There are no other messages coming through. There is a constant interference. Like white noise between us and what we know is the truth. That something, deep down, isn't right.

It's insanity. Constantly fed to us in a manner that seems completely sane. Like the hold of a narcissistic lover. Gaslit and unable to distinguish fantasy from reality. Outwardly. Inwardly. Doing something that we know does not make sense but doing it anyway. Believing something you know is not true but believing it anyway.

We have been fooled. We have allowed ourselves to be fooled. Through the use of our own beautiful language. English is one of the most complicated, multifaceted languages on the planet. One word meaning millions of things and one meaning expressed in a variety of linguistic nuances.

We have been fooled through constant, unceasing messages sent to blindsided us. To confuse and disarm us, from seeing, asking or believing whatever is real out there. Patriotism: a concept that causes us to feel useful, connected, valuable, needed. But in reality, abandons our connection and loyalty to one another in favour of the demanded, emotionally blackmailed loyalty to our country. Our state. Our government. Loyalty that marches us into illegal wars and sends our neighbours to prison for a garden party with more than six individuals in the middle of a lockdown.

The new slogan is to "be kind". Months of exposure to fearmongering, scare tactics. Incendiary headlines built to pull down any internal infrastructure, any hold, any grip on reality as we know it. Sent to destroy our resolve that the world is safe. The bus is safe. Our home is safe. Panicking in the shops and panicking in our heads, the scolding fire of hot fear spreading from our hearts across our chests and up into our mouths. Pouring, like lava, out on all those who represent 'the others'. Who represent illness and worry and death. And now we are to 'be kind'. To never second guess someone's exposure to illness or trauma as a result. What a kind and thoughtful, benevolent government we have. Reminding us that kindness is the answer. But do they want actual kindness? A society unified on communal effort for care? An elderly person able to be comforted by a visiting family or a band of unknown do-gooders?

Or is kindness really lived in complying with draconian procedures, not visiting those we love, not challenging those around us in any manner that evokes anything other than complicit thought? In ensuring that we cover our mouths (and eyes) from connecting or engaging with one another?

What was Brexit all about? How quickly we forget being lied to. 300 billion for our NHS. Weapons of mass destruction in Iraq. All bought through the use of clever wording, not quite able to be challenged through taxpayer-backed payments to spin doctors. Who ultimately avoid recourse through the clever untechnicalities of their messages.

Election and manipulation seem synonymous nowadays. So much so that we invent and revel in satires of the lies we swallow. Do we even care anymore? About what we believe or what we are made to believe?

Everything is upside down. Roundabout and inside out. Everything has an undertone, a second message, something hiding behind the dazzling lights; the temptation found in the first. Even the basics have been completely misconstrued. Completely bedraggled in their presentation and their impact. An eye for an eye. Quoted so many times in action revenge thrillers. The honourable hero, exerting his biblical rights on an evil overlord, exacting harm on unsuspecting victims. But what does it actually mean? The replacement of a sheep. Or rice. Or money. If misused. Or lost. Or killed, whilst in my possession. The repaying of my debt. Not the repaying of the devils. Not the blasphemous roll of God in deciding someone's fate. From a position of absolute ungrace.

"So turn the other cheek then", everyone says. In their benevolent, righteous, pious manner. Don't judge or berate. Be better than the last ungrateful, selfish worm who has accosted you your fortune, your pride, your ego. What kind of message is that? Because Jesus meant, "Slap me again". Because it is only through this position, this madness, the offering of your cheek for further punishment, that one can see the true message of God. That I am not better than, but here to serve you. That I will always forgive, even at my own expense. So slap me again, as I embody the grace of God, which is not calculated on deservedness, but given freely.

Especially in the face of hatred and disdain. As kindness and mercy in these times may be the only thing that penetrates a cruel and twisted, unkind heart. That is how we get the message out. Clear and far and wide.

For these are the parts of us that are God-like. Our highest thought and feeling and action. For how else would He show Himself to us in a manner that was indisputable? Indefensible. He cannot. So He sends His message through us and into others. Quietly. Steadily. With that feeling in our hearts (and evoked in others) undeniable.

Even here. My message is lost in translation. Too many interceptions, disruptions, interferences in the way to make it really feel like it means something. I'm so desperate to do good by God, to fulfil my purpose, my prophecy, I can't even think straight. I am weighed down and overcome, overwhelmed with doubt. With scarcity in my ability to deliver a message that is clear, meaningful, acceptable. To God. To myself. To others.

But I realised through writing that I can only tell my truth. The truth. Not a cleverly held together portion of what sounds good. What will sell. What I believe I should be. How I feel I will be judged. And I hope against hope that it will mean something, somewhere, to someone.

Everything we do is so completely, utterly consumed by this society, this world, that we often lose, we often forget the meaning of our own messages. We get lost, distracted and scared on the way home. We are so indebted to each other's egoistic views of ourselves that we miss the thing that makes any message truly powerful.

The feeling of it.

Search for miracles and you will find them. They are all around you. Just dulled down and made fantasy by the powers that be, so that we wouldn't recognise them as more than a Hollywood car crash. Feel your way through it. Connect with one another. And the message God is trying to show you will be right there.

We used to know it. As children. It was so simplistic. Good felt good. Bad felt bad. Now bad is cool and good is boring. Who told us this? And why? Try not to confuse yourself with the messages brought home to us by other people. People with their own agendas. Look again at your list. And look again inside. To where you are penetrated. With good. And with bad. And how *this* is the word and the truth and the way at its very core. At its base. Unfettered, uninterrupted, unsullied. Made just for your ears and just for your heart.

What then do you hear? When you are alone? When you stop and silence everything? Can you even do that? Can you switch off? Or is the comforting, constant humdrum, the constant drone, the rhetoric of others a constant background to your life? A comforting distraction to your own thoughts. To your own fears. Whose voice do you hear when you just stop? Try it now. Is it yours? Is it His? Or is it someone else's. Something else's?

What has happened to us? Where did we go? Were we ever really here? What is our purpose? What do we stand for? What do we choose? If we have nothing but free will, and this is the one thing God gave us, then where do we align it? With ourselves and our own selfish wants? Do we choose not to see what is happening around us? Or are we under duress? Incapacitated from seeing? All the years of chasing those A's, and uni applications, and the application of thoughtless regurgitation, and the teacher's admonitions of anything unfamiliar ringing in our ears. Surrounded by the constant, nonstop persecution of information. All bolstered by our need to be vindicated, to be different, to be justified. And blameless in our individualism. And too comfortable in our credit card–bought lifestyles to want to want the shift. To make the shift.

Wake up. We are wandering. In the wilderness. Trying to find the thing we lost. The thing we once knew. The meaning. The essence. The message. The truth. Incapable of hearing God, or any goodness. Any Godness, for that matter, when something else is constantly talking.

Who or what are we listening to? Who are we worshipping? Deities? False gods? Money, fame, glamour? Pride, vanity, ego? The Kardashians? Ourselves? What messages are we constantly receiving? About who we should be and what we should do? Do we do for others because we desire for their happiness? Their satisfaction. Or is it for our own sanctification? As kind. Generous. Benevolence personified? And then resent them. Those who are not grateful? Those who do not sanctify our good deeds and lack reverence for our munificence. Like all those people glorified in their charity. YouTubed with subscribers. Scripted in their graciousness. And conscripted to self-glorification.

I spent years hating God. Sneering at Him. And all those who valiantly hailed and exalted him. And now I spend days too scared to vindicate Him. To embrace my love of Him and declare my obedience. To be persecuted for His sake. To lay it all on the line and have something of my own to fight for. Something of everyone's to fight for. Fighting against myself to be the light. To be the beacon for others. Too used to and succumbed to the world we live in. The messages I receive every day when I open my phone, turn on my TV or the page of a newspaper.

Be the beacon. Trust that when you stop paying attention to what is being thrust in your face, something else will alight inside of you. When you begin to accept that there is a world. Something sacred. And important beyond our television screen. And the veiled screen we choose not to see. Trust that there is more. And you are more. And you have the capacity to set fire to this world. One lantern at a time. Be the watchtower, alerting others to impending attack. To the need to ready ourselves to fight.

Wake up. See beyond the façaded horizon. The beautiful pretence. Picturesque and inviting in its delivery. But grotesque behind its charade. Behind the thin veneer of a reality created just for us. To bind and limit us. *Truman* style. Instead, be true men. Do not be led by fear. Do not surrender to the anxiety, driven into us. Day after day. The unveiled message that we have something to fear, someone to fear. Do not perish in its wake and begin to despair for yourself and fear of your neighbour. Do not be separated. Do not be individualised. Instead, be peaceful. Be calm. Be a peacemaker. Be loving and kind. Be honourable. Be merciful and full of grace. Believe in miracles. And fairy tales. And dreams come true. Believe that there is something working for you. Just for you. For your happiness and contentment. For your glory and honour. But that it can only be found in His honour.

Use this strength. To challenge this world and speak a truth that we have all long forgotten.

That miracles are real.

And God speaks to you.

If only you will listen. If only you will put down what the world tells you you should be holding right now, quiet your busy articulate, oh-so-clever mind. Your indulging and insatiable heart. And really listen. Because he is not going to shout to get your attention. He is not going to bullishly barge into your life. He is not going to brandish and brand Himself. With sexy wording. And on-trend fashion. Hollywood blockbuster style. Clever plot lines and subterfuge meanings, where you're never quite sure who is the bad guy. And whose team you're on until it's over. A clever marketing ploy for your soul. He wants you to seek Him. To want to hear Him. To want to listen. To want to serve. Him and the family he created all around you in this world. Each and every one of us. He is waiting for you. He is running towards you. To offer you the grace only He can give. That you do not and never will deserve, but you get either way.

So, do not be so quick. Or so scared. Or so distracted. Or so fearful. Or so confused. That you do not hear His message. That you come away with the wrong things, or forget what you needed, or leave half of it behind in a befuddled, forgotten state.

Calm.

Quiet yourself.

Cut through all of the commotion.

Like a bullet through the gunpowder surrounding you.

So you can find a space where you can listen.

Because he is so close.

That to be heard.

He only has to whisper.

THE FOUR EASY-PEASY STEPS TO KNOWING THAT YOU MIGHT POSSIBLY BE POSSESSED.

1. ADMIT THERE IS A PROBLEM

I can pinpoint the moment my resolve completely failed. My heart broken and my trust shattered. Head down, greasy-haired, eyes lowered. Sat in my car, having given up. Just over a year into a relationship with someone I adored and realising again that I am not wanted, and that I am worthless, and nothing and nobody.

That sadness. That sadness, engulfed everything in me. My soul sunk into inexistence, and my walls came down. Sadness overcame me and with it something took hold. That's not to say that I had not been compromised, oppressed, under the influence throughout my life and up to that point. My childhood had made me ripe for it. Ripe for the picking. The enemy watching me. Gangs of them. Persons in their own right, highly intelligent. Watching, studying, waiting for an in. Goading me on, with grimaced glee.

Moments. All throughout my life. A moment of intense fear, being raped on that Peckham couch. And in enters fear. A feeling that never since abated. The sense that everywhere I went I was being followed, stalked. Dark alleyways and horror movies. A moment of intense loss, unworthiness. Another car passing by my bedroom window not ferrying my father. And in enters unworthiness, I lose another part of myself. A moment of intense shame, anger, unhappiness; relived and revisited a thousand times over in my childhood.

And again, absolute sadness, weakness, insignificance invading me now, as I sit in this car. Shame, anger, unworthiness, loss, unhappiness and fear. The realisation that all I have been taught, about me, the world, others, hitting me now in one clean sucker punch. If there is ever a time of vulnerability. It is now.

This is my weakest moment. My weakest place. And after it, I was never, ever fully the same. My eyes were darkened, much like my thoughts, and the compulsion to hate became typical – so much so that I didn't even notice it after a while. The torment increased and with it the background rumblings of insanity, the hatred of God and the defiling of my soul through unclean thoughts and unclean deeds. Harassed and enticed into action by something I wasn't even aware was there, wasn't even aware existed.

How could there not be a problem? I was broken, lost unaccepted and unaccepting. I was adrift in a sea of confusion, having limited understanding, insight or capacity for real, unadulterated love. How could there not be something very, very wrong with me? With the infrastructure holding me up? All the beams brandishing the trademark of neglect, abandonment, emotional abuse.

And, ironically, it's nothing more, worse or better than most in this world. This unkind world, this fast-paced world, this unrelenting world. Parental misgivings an accepted part of childhood. A rite of passage. All of us too busy, stressed, distracted, unavailable to do better. To be better. So trauma is normalised in the heat of the dog-eat-dog world we have created for ourselves.

Of course there's a problem. There's something wrong with all of us. But because there's something wrong with all of us, it looks like there's nothing wrong at all. And just like all those years of my childhood I lived inside a thoughtless vacuum, an intangible feeling. Knowing instinctively something was up, but never quite able to catch it, to put my finger on it. Just like that, now we live. Searching for meaning from one another's untouchable and intangible lives and the structure that rises up around us, like concrete buildings, erected to keep us in. To make us feel safe.

Wandering the hardened streets we stare at each other, gripping tight to the reality that everything is fine. A reality limited through its own relativity. But something is wrong. Not in what we see, or what we hear, or what we know. But in what we feel, what we sense. Even with our Facebook-scrolling, Insta-lifestyle, series-drooling, news-swallowing, dulled senses. Sick and nauseous on the sickly, bittersweetness of it all. We have to admit, something is not right.

Do you feel lonely? Do you feel unsure, scared or worried? Do you feel angry, irritated, frustrated, annoyed? Do you feel sad, empty, overcome? Are you tired, worn out, exhausted and beaten? Are you restless, like something is missing, like there's an urgency to get somewhere and you're not quite sure where, or why it's everyone else's fault you can't? Me too.

Do you have thoughts that are ugly? Against others, yourself? Against your loved ones, parents, children, friends, the postman? Do you catch yourself off guard with flashes of hatred? Worded in a manner that shocks and appals even you? Do you find yourself lost at times, carried away; spirited away in thoughts about you and everyone else? Comparisons and contrition and condemnation towards either, or both? Me too.

Do you want it all? Do you greed and lust and covet what you can't have? What you can have? What you already have? What you deserve and everything that everyone else has but you? Do you define and redefine yourself? As something better, something worse, or something different? Do you need that Facebook like, that friend accept, that Insta heart? Does it fill your heart, instantly, with happiness and cruel, envious vanity? Is your ego starving, crying out for attention, and to be fed with a constant, nonstop nourishment of validating information. About your place in the world and everyone else's? Me too.

Do you drink, do you smoke, do you swear? Do you take recreational drugs? Do you wear short skirts, show your skin, flash your muscles, fuck for the sake of it? Do you sleep with your partner consistently without being married? Do you flirt, do you tease, do you like the attention? Do you watch porn and TV series about power, madmen, thrones and games that are nothing more than porn regenerated? Do you fight? Do you ruckus, do you affray on a night out, just to feel alive? Me too.

We are sick. We are all sick. Compelled. Harassed. Enticed. Tormented, enslaved and defiled every moment of every day. Deceived as to the righteousness of our positions in this world, rather than as the Father sees us. And the derivation of it all. We have been compromised from the moment we picked that apple from the tree and killed ourselves with knowledge. Broken from it.

And the craziest thing is not that we did it, knowing that we would surely die. Not that the moment that we became aware of right and wrong we judged ourselves and each other. Not that through judgement and condemnation we consistently feel unworthy of God's grace, constantly question and reject the notion that no matter what we do, He loves us anyway – it is completely counterintuitive to the constructs we have created around us. And it's not that we opened ourselves up to sin and death and damnation, through just knowing what it was.

The craziest thing is that God knew we were going to eat from that tree when he planted it. And He did it anyway. So much like the Oracle and Neo. Would we ever have known what we were and what we could be? Would we ever have strived for it again, if we never lost it in the first place? Because it is only through the comparison of who we are, who we actually are, that we know who we actually are.

But in this world, the world where the tree is long forgotten as folk myth, we are fighting a constant battle where we open ourselves over and over again to the enemy, to all those persons, sent here by the father of lies himself, homeless and seeking refuge, lurking all around us.

So, admit that there is a problem. Not just you. But you and you and you as well. Admit there is a problem, and it becomes not yet another shameful disgrace in the long list of shameful disgraces, but a salvation, a beacon, a buoy. Something that can begin to truly distinguish us from them and thus, protect us from those who seek to attack and deceive and derail us.

Admit there is a problem and in it find peace and power and authority over the things that are harboured inside of you.

Admit there is a problem and with it confront society and your place within it. Take back control. Build back your infrastructure. Find a new rite of passage. And with it a new truth, a new way. A new life.

2. ADMIT THAT THE PROBLEM IS NOT EVERYONE ELSE.

Displacement, transference and countertransference. A lot of different terms for blaming someone else for your shit. I spent years, literally years doing it. For every situation I found myself in, another person was to blame. Even now, I border on the blame culture I am indoctrinated in. My mum, my dad, Thomas Robertson, Phia Eastown, the exes, the baby daddies, the courts, Courtney. All of them.

I can remember, well, all the times I denied anything was wrong. Even when I hadn't showered for over a week and when my face was harassed at the stress of keeping it contorted into something that resembled normal, approachable. The strain held around my eyes, wide and distraught, beleaguered and under siege from an enemy unknown. A wicked and shamed, wide-eyed expression constantly on my face.

I remember telling Courtney once, when he could clearly see, and sense, and hear, and see I was very unwell, that I had to keep my face like this. To save it and all those who looked at it from the sunken, depressed, greying, broken face that was hidden behind that thinned, crazed mask.

I can remember being determined to say I was OK, at least some of the time. Because I couldn't say I was ill, I was struggling, I was losing every day. But I *was* ill every day. I was struggling and losing. I was tired. I lived sad, sunken, depressed. My stomach hurt all the time, and my head was filled to bursting.

But I could never admit it. Because for much of my illness – my possession – I wasn't even aware that it wasn't me. I was so focussed on him, on everyone else. Courtney's drug use, his terrible lack of care, his lack of financial restraint, his neglect of my needs, his cheating, his autonomy over his own life. His confidence in himself and God.

And my complete lack of freedom, my burden, my kids, my house, my responsibilities. My parents and all they had deprived me of. Yes, because of the myriad of intrusions in my head, my inability to see the wood from the trees. But mainly because I didn't want to see it. I didn't want to admit it. I knew it. Somewhere in the space between my head and my heart, but to believe it could be possible that I was causing not only everyone else's, but, God forbid it, my own misery was a burden way too heavy to bear.

So the burden of my circumstances, and the burden of my relationship, and the burden of my past became an easier yoke to carry, despite it breaking my back and my resolve day by day.

I was determined. Determined to struggle on. In the belief that there was nothing I could do to change my situation and that my salvation lived in the hands of others. How right I was, but how wrong I had it. I often think back to the shame I felt throughout that time. The constant, unending, nagging feeling that I was ashamed and shameful. This feeling that sank each day, each breath and each swallow into the pit of my stomach, slowly built up layer after layer until I could taste its bitter stench again.

Of the shame, of my actions, my thoughts, my deeds. My vileness, iniquity and disgustingness. Disgusted in myself. But moreover, the shame that lived in the secret, the internal/eternal secret, that if it wasn't anyone else. It was me. And I was powerless to change it. The magnitude of my position, my illness, my evilness; well, if it was me, I was fucked. And plus. It meant it was me. All the thoughts, all the flashes of pure evil, all the dreams, every nasty, hateful, scornful, vengeful thought I had. I owned. My complete lack of motivation. My constant tiredness, the mess of my house and the fact that I couldn't stand my own children, my own self at times. Well, that was all me.

And no-one, no-one else could save me. Because it was no-one else's fault. How scary. How completely overwhelmingly, undefinedly fearful I was each day. And at each juncture, it almost looked like it might, just might, be me that was responsible for it all.

Whole nights spent with Courtney spelling out, literally spelling out to me why I was seeing things strange, why my view was off, why he wasn't wholly to blame. And I still had managed to convince him the majority of our failing relationship was solely, complete and utterly his fault.

But it was preferable that I was blameless and therefore, had and maintained the power. Over the alternative reality I had created and now forced everyone to live in. Fuelled by a desperation to not have to look into the mirror, preferring to inhabit this mirrored reality.

It's so easy. To run away, to sprint into blamelessness. In an attempt to protect yourself from the pain, the blame, the shame, the responsibility and the hard work of change. It's OK though. Go ahead. Forgive yourself and move on to the next step. Everything will be OK. Because you are stronger than you know.

3. ADMIT THAT THE PROBLEM IS, IN FACT, YOU.

OK. So it's you. How unfortunate. How horrific. How disarming. What a shit show. So, every time you've thought they don't like you, they're talking about you, they're laughing at you. Courtney doesn't love you, that he's probably cheating. That nothing is fair, how cruel and exhausting your life is and how you could just pack it all in. That was you. Every time you've caught yourself reminiscing, revelling even, on some shameful embarrassment. That was you. Every time horrific images of all description, of the past, the future and all things that have never and will never happen play across the screen of your mind. Every time. That was you.

All the vengeful hatred and the bile that comes up from your stomach into your throat, every restrained negative comment. Every part of your life that you are ungrateful for, everything you look at with disdain and disgust. All the things you not only don't appreciate, but physically reject as a burden, as another self-pitying stance. All of it. It was all you. It's not, "the others", it's not society, it's not the world. It just little old, negative, unhappy, ungrateful, undeserving you.

What a mind fuck. Finally having removed all of the obstacles in your way. Finally having had them removed for you, Courtney and all the others refusing to offer sanctuary for you to rest your blame within. The slow, yet shocking instantaneous realisation sinking into your mind, that you, and only you, own these feelings and these thoughts and your own unhappiness. What an absolute mind fuck.

So are you powerless then? Are you defeatist and defeated? If it's not the world, unjustly and unfairly exacting its cruelty into you and you are the one behind it all, turning the cogs and operating the machinery, then surely you can choose something else. Right?

I remember scrambling for reason over this period. For inspiration. Finally realising that I was not a victim in this world and finally resisting the natural urge to lay the responsibility for it all at everyone else's door. And I remember flailing. Completely lost about how to make a change. Never having even considered it as a viable option before. Searching and scrambling, not for meaning anymore, but for movement. Listening with intent and expectation, for myself and not for him, to Courtney's sermons to me on change, his lectures, his suggestions and inspiration. Finally seen for what they were. A tool designed to save me from myself. Inspiration eventually he could never aspire to, but that engineered and marked out a road for me out of the chaos.

And I remember failing. Over and over. Constantly and consistently. And being broken all over again, my newly found optimisms wavering firstly, finally strewn aside and tarnished. Until eventually my failure became impossible to ignore. I couldn't fix myself. If anything, I was worse. I was more unhappy, more vengeful, more scornful, more tormented. More powerless and hopeless with every passing day. Suicide slowly crept in as the only likely cure. Driven insane by the recognition of my situation, my role, through the desire to change and the inability to make even a dent.

I recovered and relapsed within weeks, days, hours sometimes. Never quite able to hold onto reality, to gratitude, to positivity. And I became completely disparaging, completely despondent, downhearted and desperate and completely alone in my struggle. It was no longer a journey, destination unknown. There was a clear and deliberate destination in mind. One I felt I deserved and all would benefit from. Death beckoned like a beautiful relief from the constant pain I was in. Somehow alight and relit from the realisation that I couldn't blame all that lived around me. Like a veil pulled back, only to reveal a much uglier truth. One written in indelible ink.

A realisation dawned that I was sick. Very sick. With no foreseeable cure. No remedy. No pain relief. And only one sure-fire way to end it all. To end it all.

How lonely that place is. No matter how much Courtney tried to hold onto me, it was like he was gripping the ghost of my past. The memory of me that was only able to live in this world because (1) this heresy was not me, (2) I couldn't do anything about it, or (3) that it was me and I was able to elicit change.

No one could have reached me, no one could have touched me, brought me back from the brink. From watching myself in the sunken place. No one but Him. But my God. Watching on in agony of His own, for my torture, my pain. For my complete unawareness of what was truly happening to me.

That, yes, this mind lived within this body. Yes, this sounded like my voice in my head. Yes, this was my screen images played across. On repeat. Yes, everything appeared in order, although completely and utterly out of order. But like a sheep in wolf's clothing, I was covered, cloaked in something else. There was another person here with me. Here within me. Always. Something that would never be seen at first glance but inhabited my entire being, save for the small, almost diminished spark of me still longing to be good, still longing to remember me, still longing for me. Still fighting for me.

That the 'you' who had accepted responsibility for it all, was in fact not me.

And knowing I would never be able to see what was behind my own eyes, them currently being used and abused by the enemy.

He came.

To show me and to save me.

4. ADMIT THAT, IN TRUTH, IT'S NOT YOU. AT ALL.

So, let's get down to it. What is evil? What is demon? What is possession?

Note to reader: I have titled this chapter *Admit*, and I say Admit That, in Truth, It's Not You at All because it is an admission, it is something extremely brave, courageous and ambitious in admitting these things to oneself. Something that tears down the very fabric of your existence and rebuilds it with something ridiculous and scary and completely unbelievable. Improbable, but not impossible.

Because there are, whether you wish to believe it or not, two separate and distinct realms. Two separate realities, that exist side by side, within and without of one another. Two realms that represent two sides of the same coin. Real and unreal. And in both of these realms there is good and bad. God and *evil*.

It's a hard term to swallow. It's not really dinner party material and has long been relegated to the realm of myth and legend by most. Even those who read and study the Bible, believe in Jesus and all his works and the magnificence and glory of the Father; even those, at large, don't believe in demons as an actual physical thing. A thing that occupies the world in the same manner as we do, but rather relates the exorcism of multiple Jews by Jesus and his disciples as more of a metaphorical state of being. A 'demonic psyche' if you like. All of the negative thoughts and feelings and actions psychologically extracted, like a Rogerian Doctorated Messiah. Well, Jesus was humanistic at his core, I guess.

And if that's the limit of the believer's stance, what chance do the rest of us have?

Demons and demonic possession were not things I ever believed in. These were not things I ever thought about. Like most, I chalked it up to a fictional fanatical horror-based fantasy. Something to tell naughty children and those who needed to be kept in line by the Bible bashers. A religious bogeyman, if you like. Lying in wait, under the bed, for your sinful feet to touch the floor.

The Bible, Jesus, God, all of it, wasn't something I had studied or thought about in any great manner, other than to dismiss the likelihood of a God with my carefully placed intellectual wit. Therefore, it came as quite a shock to me that I had, in fact, been possessed, or had an evil spirit, or several for that matter, inhabiting the same space as me.

I have done some research on what I experienced since, still thirsting to satisfy the analytic of my brain, that can't quite rationalise my experiences in full, if at all. What I've learnt is that demons, unclean spirits, or evil entities are in fact not much different to you and me, in that they inhabit the earth, and even if they cannot be fully seen or heard, they can nonetheless be felt. Be sensed. But in the manner that you or I are both individuals, with individual personalities and characteristics, so are demons.

They are persons in their own right. Persons, however, unlike us, that do not have a safe space to dwell do not have a home of their own, but are in fact homeless. Bodyless and ultimately, soulless. Individuals with differing behaviours, and highly intelligent, supernaturally intelligent really. They watch us, study us, despise us. For having something they never, ever knew, or once knew but gave up for something they were deceived into believing had more value. They know us, possibly better than we know ourselves – having been there from the beginning. Watching, waiting, imitating. Intently studying each of us, as well as having an expertise in human behaviour, human failure. Our temptation and sin. They are well adept to entice and deceive us.

Still with me? Still intrigued? Still disbelieving and dismissive?

So, as persons sent by Lucifer, the enemy, the deceiver, the father of all lies. The devil. A man – a fallen angel – so jealous of us and how we are loved, forgiven, exalted by a God that would never do the same for his own transgressions. An entity so envious of God's position and power, but not His mercy and grace, that he seeks to defile and steal all those who grace the potential to love Him and live in His name. A thing so bitter and so completely blinded by his own role and importance to the story of God, of us. Created by God so that He could know definitively, conclusively, absolutely that He is goodness, that He is love. So bitter that his every action seeks to sever our own awareness of who we are, in God's likeness, to ensure that we never, ever achieve our own destiny and purpose. As who God made us to be.

This guy. This guy sends out his minions for two distinct purposes. Firstly, to stop us from ever knowing God, ever believing He exists. And upon failing in their first objective – and this is for all the Christians out there, pious and litigious in their worship – fractures and contorts our relationship and view of God respectively and ensures that we never become effective Christians anyway.

"So how?" I hear you ask. I hear you sneer, "How do these so-called demons possess and oppress you?" Well, firstly, there is a distinct difference between oppression and possession. *Oppression*, as a definition, is "the exercise of authority or power in a burdensome, cruel or unjust manner", "the feeling of being heavily burdened, mentally or physically". I personally don't understand the difference between oppression or possession (those more well-read than me informing that there is no coming back from possession by the devil), having had the shadow of another person ripped from my body and the shadow of another's thoughts, feeling, deeds, desires and mental, emotional and physical torments shadowing my own mind.

But I know that this feeling is equivalent to the feeling of a heavy burden, an unjust, cruel, burdensome authority. With complete authority.

It's difficult to really explain. Like depression, anxiety, or any mental health condition, I suppose. Or what it feels like to break a leg, or a heart. But I do recall my mind being full. Full to the absolute brim with constant, nonstop, never-ending, uninterrupted, incessant talking. Constant noise. My own voice never, ever, ever letting up. It was like standing as a small child in a silent and vacuous room, neck craned and staring upwards, surrounded by tall, dark, faceless shadowed things towering over me. I was crowded in and couldn't see much past a row or two deep, but I knew these things filled the entire space and they were fighting, grabbing, reaching over each other to get to me. And even though I couldn't see them, I could sense they had something vacant inside them, something different to what I could feel inside me

– like a grey lead ball to a shining golden snitch – and they all sounded just like me. And I was pretty much convinced it was me, but I couldn't quite see, and everything was grey.

And all they do is tell you how stupid and ridiculous and pathetic you are. All they do is comment, constantly, on every action you take, every sentence you utter and all the other thoughts that you, as that small child, hesitate to make. They second-guess all your decisions and remind you all the time that you are a joke, worthless, laughable. They laugh at you and scorn you and point their bony, twisted fingers at you. Into you, through you.

They play you 4D replays of all the times you've felt pain and shame and desperation. Every time you've needed, cried out for someone and found yourself alone. They relate every action you take in this world, down to cutting the veg for dinner, to some shameful regret, or some painful atrocity inflicted upon you by another.

Remember that time you were cooking? Remember when you were cutting veg? Remember it was when Courtney had left, again, to go out with his friends, again, to take a load of drugs, again, to care about himself again. Remember how he's never here to help? Remember all the other times he's let you down? Remember when he cheated? Oh, that hurts, doesn't it? Remember! How pathetic are you? Still here, cutting veg for him. Plus, here, have some images. Him stroking her arm, her face. Lying next to her. Both of them. Laughing together. Laughing at you. You're a laughingstock. That's right. Tell him. Tell him how you hate him. And loathe him. And despise him. How the very sight of him makes your skin crawl. Tell him! But wait. You're too pathetic, too scared to do that. Too useless and small and pathetic and scared. So, seethe. Rage and seethe inside instead. Cry for yourself, you loser. But never for him. Fuck him. And his dinner. And that girl. What a tramp. What a whore. Both of them. They deserve each other. You hate him. Don't you? And whose fault is it? Who let it happen to them? You joke, you pathetic loser. But you should probably stir the dinner. Or it'll burn. And the kids won't eat. Because no one else is going to feed them. Are they? No. It's just you. Alone. Stuck. And drowning in it all. And do they care, or appreciate it? Fucking ungrateful kids. No. No they don't. Just fucking end it. For you or for them. Fuck 'em anyway. Fuck 'em all. I can't wait til I'm alone.

But I was never alone. And it never stopped. It was unceasing. A constant, never-ending attack of words, thoughts, pictures, feelings. The feeling of being weighed down was with me constantly. I was never free, or light, or excited about anything. I woke up tired and sick of everything. I had a constant feeling of unease and felt trapped. All the time.

That just sounds like depression I hear you say. Or bipolar. Or multiple personality syndrome. Until you're saved and you realise that your voice has a strange undertone, a hiss, a rasp to it that distorts the sound ever so slightly, like a speaker with a wire loose. Until you realise that every thought you thought was your own actually originated from behind your right ear. Until you realise that you never seemed to talk about yourself in the first person. And never had the comparison until you were well. Back. Here. Present.

Because I was sick. Very, very unwell. So much so I was driven to contemplating suicide. Only it was nothing conventional, in what is currently considered conventional, that saved me. Nothing pathology could cure. Maybe you think me just weak? Easily influenced. But by who then? By what? Because all of these voices sounded like my own. These images lived in my head, these feelings in my gut. I wasn't aware that I was under siege. Because this is, unquestionably, the first and most fundamental trick of the devil. To make you believe that he does not exist. And through this deception, my hate and my anger and sorrow were claimed by me and me alone. I and I alone taking ownership for my own mental, emotional, and physical state. And through this simple yet effective trick, this easy and acceptable lie, how easily was I compelled to hate others and pity myself. And hate myself and pity others' attempts at love. How easily was I tormented, driven insane with the belief I was going crazy. How easily was I enticed into defiling myself through the daily, hourly, minute-by-minute harassment. As these are the tools used by those sent by the enemy to entice, enslave, torment, compel, defile, harass and deceive you. Until you are enslaved by it all.

That doesn't sound like me, you may think. Well, no, these are my predilections. Not yours. Because, if God is not even capable of heavily influencing your actions, because He gave you one defining feature, so that you might know what it means to love Him, freely. In His gift of free will. Your freedom to decide at your own will what you do and do not choose, or what privilege you exercise even at His expense. So, if even God, the creator, omnipotent, omnipresent and omniscient, can't force you, then certainly neither can Lucifer.

These persons are, however, as I have discussed, highly intelligent beings, who study you, watch you and learn what you do and how you react and what you react to. And watching in wait, find that thing, that one thing, that is the least godly: anger, sorrow, addiction, depression, or whatever it might be. And circle you. In times of high stress, heightened desire, infatuation, addiction, sorrow, hurt, pain, loss, sadness. They wait until your lowest, highest, maddest, saddest moment, and at the second you have lost yourself, even for the briefest of moments, they enter and they dwell there. And from that moment on you will never be quite the same. There is something there that wasn't there before or something that you had that is now lost. A glint in your eye or a tone, a gravel to your voice. Or a compulsion that you can't quite control. And they amplify the feeling you already have. The failures you have already lived. All the justifications you already make. Or the ego, or vanity, or self-love, self-pity, self-distress. That always lived there. They take whatever it is and amplify it. They take what you believe to be you and use it to deceive and control you. Under the clever guise of free will. The unquestionable façade of your own mind, body and soul. Until you lose yourself, finally either at best succumbing to, or at worst revelling in, who you are now. Or drowning in the disappointment of it all.

For me, it was and still is shame. I still find myself now. Even with all my knowledge and the authority I have found in Jesus, and the comfort and safety I have found in God. Even with all this, I still find myself under serious and immobilising oppression. Shame always being the road in. Because we are constantly under spiritual warfare. It begins and ends in our minds, if we let it. And starts with simply saying no.

Recognising what is happening to you and standing your ground. Seeking help from Jesus and deciding that these things have no power over you. Because you are a child of God.

So once again! I don the armour given to me. The truth. That this is real. That God exists. Righteousness. That I am unconditionally loved, even when I do not deserve it. Faith. That I am saved, and safe. Salvation. In my soul, believed in my head and my heart. And the spirit embodied in your own body, which once there, nothing else can be. And finally, in the word of God. Which if studied and understood holds the truth and the power of all.

And Grace . . .

We generally remember God on our deathbeds, recounting all our fears and follies as we pray heartily for salvation in the sudden clarity eternity brings. Other than this, most only think of God during life for a few reasons: to plead for miracles in times of need or to barter for our utmost desires in the face of adversity, only to immediately and instinctively forget answered prayers once received; in our consistent and overriding belief that God could never truly exist – considering the absolute carnage and devastation around the globe. The unfairness of prosperity through iniquity, the complete injustice of murder, rape, brutality, and offshore bank accounts. The horrific, maniacal truth and lunacy that there could ever be allowed such evil to exist, in the presence of anything as almighty as The Almighty.

But what if it didn't need to be like this? What if God's name was not dragged through the proverbial trials of morality and fairness and subjective context? What if God just smote them all? Them, of course. Not you. Or me. Because surely this is where God will draw the distinction between good and bad, and right and wrong, and heaven and hell. And we all know exactly which side of history we would be on. Right? The same side of history we have always been on. Right? As individuals above reproach. Surely then, we would break less of a sweat and wring our hands a little looser upon our deathbeds.

And all would be right in the world. The clear distinction found by God in all His glory and wisdom will have uprooted all evil, all inequity, all wrongdoing, and equality would finally reign supreme. And we would rejoice that there truly is a God. We would rejoice in our own salvation, once again turning on – I mean to – one another to validate our goodness, through no less than the vindication offered through the new emerging comparisons, now budding in the natural order of a balance-seeking organism. And all, including each and every one of us, would be right. Drop mic. Exit left.

Believe me, God has tried. And tested. Each method. The total destruction of Sodom and Gomorrah, the law as imposed by Moses, including no less than an engineer-level altar design for the sacrifice of our sins by the Great Engineer, to the legalistic foibles of the Pharisees. God has punished, and warned, and shouted, and sent us to our rooms, all to no avail. God has burnt the whole goddam house down and then flooded it for good measure. Just to allow us the opportunity to start anew. And much like a keen and anxious father, like the humble and considerate father He is, He takes stock of what works. And what clearly does not. It has been a period of trial and error, but, hey, no one gives you a handbook on creating the multiverse. Sometimes you just have to make it up as you go.

So how, then, do you find balance? Order, over millennia? Fairness for each and every individual in their individual moment in time, throughout time and space, within the linear concept said individual can comprehend it as? How do you love fairly? Treat fairly? Give fairly? How do you define and value and devalue the lives and experiences, the losses, and the pain of one human being against another? How do you account for the behaviour, both born of and beholden to, the pain of one person? And condone? Or save? How do you make it all right, for all persons, over all time? How do you allow for the poor experiences, the poor thought processes, the poor choices and the poor actions that generate greatness and understanding and growth whilst simultaneously preserving perfect and accountable equilibrium for all? Where do you draw the line, who do you choose, who do back and who do you knock back? What's the policy? And who does it serve?

People always say, "If you could walk a mile in my shoes". But those shoes I wouldn't want the responsibility of filling. And yet, despite, God knows my every step and watches on with care and tender, loving grace. Unconditional in His understanding and empathy at each faltered step. At each dragged foot. At each footprint left. Immovable in his readiness to embrace, each time we cross the threshold onto the other side. As He sits in all sides. In all corners.

Because this is the only way. This is the only way the system can thrive. Not only is all in absolute balance over the vastness of eternity. Not only do we need the dark for the light to be seen. Not only are we cultivating and reliving experiences to surely develop within this and the next lives, and not only is it impossible to inhabit a system of comparative morality without consistently falling short or being perennially confused as to what we truly represented in each given moment.

Not only all of the above – as well as the gift of grace being offered indiscriminately, blindly and broadly – the devotion of such grace offered to us is not ours to give and therefore, how can we possibly dictate who and how, and when, and where, and how much is given to us? Grace is the ultimate get-out-of-jail-free card. No doubles, no payment, no soul. Given to us by a God who truly understands why. And through this, it is offered unreservedly and indiscriminately and in equal measures to all who ask for it. And many who don't. As, just like a child instinctively forgives all who appeal, and invariably becomes vulnerable in the process, so is our God in the face of us and we in the face of Him.

Yet the freedom to choose, the biggest gift of grace God could muster, remains a much-misconstrued concept to man, its symptomatic disorder so often utilised to dismiss, attack and annihilate the very existence of the giver of the gift. Hailed as evidence of His absence altogether. The idea that God will not simply intervene, in either respect, naturally results in queries around His use. Yet it is this very concept, this very love, that allows for the free will to destroy and the free will to create. And the free will to know Him, should you so choose. With no strings. Despite it being something to God that is likely a most-honoured treasure. And yet although much of His treasure chest remains plundered and empty, the grace of empathy, the grace of forgiveness and the grace of freedom are yours to love Him for or not.

So, what will you do with it?

Because there is still a battle. There are those who have taken this beautiful gift and used it to break and mould the system to their advantage and many who remain ignorant and asleep to it. There is, despite all being equal over time, good and evil; and the continued pretence that nothing more than this, than you, than me and my selfish needs exists. And it is with the belief of there being no real good that it is even easier to defunct the possibility of real evil being alive in our world. And it is through this evil attaching itself to those who's free will has led them to pain and suffering, distress and disease, bitterness and detachment, the battle rages on.

And even though their actions are forgivable, as God gave all the grace of their own free will, it is only through an acknowledgement of evil's existence that we can truly flood light onto this darkness and bring it into the light. As this is where it wants to be, whether it knows it or not. It cries out from the darkness. This is why it spends so much energy concealing itself, ironic as it may seem. As, arguably, one who cares not where it exists, light or dark, does not spend such effort deflecting, suspending and distorting the other option. Thou does project too much.

But what are we projecting? And how do we forgive those who sin against this world, who create this battle we fight within and sully the good name of free-will and grace? How do we know which side we're even on? How do we share this message and the power of God and each and every one of us? How do we give light and love when we still battle? Outwardly and inwardly.

Because I still battle. I still wake at night terrified of things I can't see. I am still quick to anger and fail in my steadfast love for others or faithfulness in the Lord. I still sin. I still have moments when I know I am being taken over and allow it, despite all my clever words and all my clever deeds and all my knowledge and power. I still suffer and cause suffering. I am still ashamed and vain and prideful and cruel and vengeful and sorrowful and lacking and selfish and self-indulged.

And through all of this it becomes hard, hard to remember that there is *nothing* that you or I could do that makes us shameful, disgusting, undesirable or intolerable in the eyes of God. And no matter what, He sees us as our most perfect and beautiful selves *whenever* He looks our way.

That He never strays from knowing exactly what we were made for. All of us. In His Image. That His grace, unbounded and completely deserved, is given freely to us as a beautiful, unattainable, unrepaybackable gift. Something that has cost the giver everything and the receiver nothing. Something indescribable and incomprehensible. Something that can move mountains and change the course of history.

As it is only through this that He melts the heart. And the resolve. And the shame. And the guilt and the condemnation of all those who receive it. It is only through this that we can create a new world, a world of love. Where fear and spite and greed and envy remain lost in the annals of another dimension that can no longer touch this new world.

Because love and beautiful, sincere, unapologetic, all encapsulating, timeless grace to one another reigns supreme.

Want some?

You already have it.

Thank Him for it.

Even though you did nothing to earn it. Even though you're a fuck-up. Even though you have turned away from Him and live and revel in the darkness. Turn back. Repent. Ask. Knock. Thank Him for it, and it will be yours.

So what will you do with it?

Will you choose again?

16 January 2021

When I think about the privilege it was to go through this experience. And to continue to walk the tightrope that is light and dark. To tiptoe along the precipice of darkness knowing you could be dragged in at any moment and the only thing that can save you is the light? So, you achingly, earnestly, eternally search for the light? What a privilege.

Amen.

Printed in Great Britain
by Amazon